ABOUT THE AUTHOR

Andreas Souvaliotis founded the world's first eco-rewards program, Green Rewards, and went on to create the popular Carrot Rewards health and wellness app. A prolific writer and public speaker, Souvaliotis is a prominent Canadian advocate for innovative approaches to social change, particularly in the areas of public health, climate change, inclusion and diversity. He holds a bachelor of science and an MBA degree and is a classically trained musician, avid cyclist and global citizen. In 2018 he was appointed Chair of Diversity and Inclusion for the Young Presidents' Organization Canada. He was born in Athens, Greece, and lives in Toronto with his partner, Joe.

MISFiT

MISFiT

autistic. gay. immigrant. changemaker.

a memoir

ANDREAS SOUVALIOTIS

DOUBLEDAY CANADA

Doubleday Canada and colophon are registered trademarks of Penguin Random House Canada Limited

Library and Archives Canada Cataloguing in Publication

Souvaliotis, Andreas, 1963-, author
    Misfit / Andreas Souvaliotis.

Previously published by the author in 2013.
Issued in print and electronic formats.
ISBN 978-0-385-69269-4 (softcover).—ISBN 978-0-385-69270-0 (EPUB)

    1. Souvaliotis, Andreas, 1963-. 2. Social entrepreneurship.
3. Entrepreneurship—Social aspects. 4. Social change. I. Title.

HD60.S68 2019   658.4'08   C2018-904931-6
                                         C2018-904932-4

Cover and book design: Leah Springate
Cover image: andersboman/Getty Images

Printed and bound in the USA

Published in Canada by Doubleday Canada,
a division of Penguin Random House Canada Limited

www.penguinrandomhouse.ca

10 9 8 7 6 5 4 3 2 1

Penguin
Random House
DOUBLEDAY CANADA

To my Joe,
the proudest, gentlest, wisest and
most unrelenting nurturer of difference.

CONTENTS

Storytelling has always been one of our species' simplest but most beautiful and effective developmental tools. We share and show and guide one another through our stories. Stories help us find how to belong, they help us learn faster and they so often help us leapfrog over a moment of self-doubt or pain.

Andreas's very human story ignites a range of emotions as you travel through this unique memoir. You feel his bewilderment as a marginalized and oddly gifted kid; you shudder sympathetically for an isolated gay teenager in a society that wasn't quite ready for him; and you definitely feel his overwhelming excitement about arriving, discovering, creating and succeeding in a new world that embraced him so openly.

His message is straightforward and powerful: harness the things that make you different in order to change your world for the better. We're all misfits, with our own particularities. And, in our quest to fit in and live "normal," we too often quash those very things that could make us special.

Andreas is a changemaker. By caring enough and by not being afraid to be different, he became one of our country's more outspoken, passionate and recognized eco-entrepreneurs.

His inspiring, colourful and uniquely Canadian story will hopefully entertain you, spark your imagination, stretch your appetite for life and multiply your desire to stand out and contribute to your tribe.

—Justin Trudeau and Sophie Grégoire

The Rt. Hon. Adrienne Clarkson
Co-Founder and Co-Chair
Institute for Canadian Citizenship

John Ralston Saul
Co-Founder and Co-Chair
Institute for Canadian Citizenship

We are thrilled that Andreas is making a gift of his royalties from this book to the 6 Degrees program. It shows the commitment and enthusiasm for the work we are doing from this remarkable and remarkably engaged citizen!

6 Degrees, whether in Toronto, Calgary or Berlin, is an amazing initiative. Andreas became part of its creation and remarkable growth in 2015. And it must be said that his ideas, experience and insights have helped immeasurably with our work. Today, thousands of people come from around the world to take part in our 6 Degrees gatherings.

We all know that racism and fear are on the rise everywhere. 6 Degrees is increasingly seen internationally as the place where a new language—a new discourse on immigration, refugees, citizenship, diversity and belonging—is being developed. That is, a discourse not dictated by fear.

6 Degrees is a grassroots movement and Andreas is a grassroots example of how citizenship can and should work.

We are all very lucky that somebody like Andreas came to Canada, to Manitoba, to Brandon to attend their wonderful university. Yes, the winters are very real, but he also discovered that the winters throw people together. Andreas is the ultimate people person. He has a fantastic loyalty to the city, to the province and to Canada.

Nobody could love Canada more than Andreas. His enthusiasm for who we are is tied into his identity and his sense of himself as a joyous Greek who has found—like Odysseus—a safe haven, in Toronto.

Andreas's life—his adventure!—his second life is in this book. We would all be foolish to think that immigration is easy because he makes it look easy. What we learn about in these pages is the adversity Andreas has had to both live with and overcome, in part thanks to his energy, imagination and decisiveness. This has made him what he is.

But then, you will discover all of this about him as you read this remarkable book.

And please, join with Andreas and ourselves. Get involved in 6 Degrees.

www.6degreesto.com

@6DegreesTO

WHY

I AM DIFFERENT. I have always been different. I grew up scared of being found out, scared of my natural inability to fit in, to conform, to look and sound and dress and behave "normal." I was always drawn to the different ones and I observed them with fascination—but the thought of being even a little bit like them mortified me. I was desperate to fit in.

It took me a very long time to grow up. The relentless pursuit of "normal" continued to dominate my life until not that long ago. My fear of being found out ruled over my childhood, my adolescence, my twenties, thirties and most of my forties. I was terrified of rejection and I always linked any form of it (from bad customer service to losing an employee to fighting with a lover) back to who and how I was. I stretched myself all the time so I could blend in—and found the effort exhausting and demoralizing. And nothing ever really changed, I felt: I fit in as poorly at forty-five as I had at five.

But then something remarkable happened: I call it "audience response." As my life and career took an unexpected turn in my mid-forties, and as I wrapped all my passion around a cause, I suddenly found my own voice. I stood on public podiums, wrote for newspapers and magazines, debated with leading authorities, preached to followers and discovered an enormous source of fuel within me. Not only did I stand out, not only was I different, more passionate, more outspoken, more intense, more bizarre and much more controversial than those "normal" people on the other side of the podium—I was also less afraid than they were. It was incredible: one day I was (or at least thought I was) the biggest lover of convention and conformity, and the next day I was carrying a flag and didn't even care to count how many were following me.

It all happened in a flash. On a beautiful spring morning in 2007, sitting in my backyard and licking my wounds from a spectacular career derailment, I came up with a big idea—and I found myself contemplating the most daring and unconventional pursuit of my life. My strange genes had already helped create a thousand jagged edges in my career trajectory, but nothing close to the wild turn I was about to take.

At a time when others were still trying to figure out this new "green" thing and understand how climate change would reshape the business world, I accidentally became one of the earliest eco-entrepreneurs in my country. I invented something. I triggered a mini revolution within my industry and inspired all sorts of brilliant minds to follow me on a wild adventure. By blending my powerful (some would say uncontrollable) desire to change the world with everything I knew about influencing human behaviour, I created the world's first rewards program for responsible lifestyle choices. Somehow, maybe by pure luck or maybe through weirdly wired brain advantage, I landed on that idea before anyone else—and that, in turn, fuelled my permanent appetite for even more disruption and even less conformity. The dream and the venture turned into a bigger dream and bigger ventures, and kept snowballing for years. Along the way I grew into a very public evangelizer, proudly sharing the tale of how magnificent it is to stumble into that magical intersection of passion and skill. I had finally discovered my hidden ability to bring a little bit of change to the world, my world.

My story isn't especially profound. I am not a psychologist, and this book contains absolutely no scientific theories or facts; it's just a simple human case study. It is the story of how a different, autistic, gay, immigrant, geeky, marginalized kid suddenly, and almost accidentally, discovered his real purpose in this world, and how that discovery enabled him to repurpose the sum of his unique attributes—eccentricities, skills, fears and passions—into a changemaker's toolkit. Once the realignment had begun, the rest happened quite naturally.

Nor is my story unique. Every one of us has what it takes to trigger a bit of change in the world; the only difference is that some people know this, and others mistakenly see their differences and quirks as handicaps.

Enjoy my weird story. I hope it inspires you to discover and harness your own edges.

NUMBERS

THEY GATHERED ALL THE STUDENTS in the school-yard, and then my Grade 1 teacher took me by the hand, walked with me up to the small balcony and told the kids how incredible it was that their young schoolmate had just been on TV. My face felt warm and I kept touching the funny powder that had caked nicely onto my cheeks and forehead. I squinted in the bright sunshine and tried really hard not to look back at all the pairs of eyes staring at me.

It was March 1970, and I was six years old. My dad had just driven me back to school from the Greek national TV studios, where I had been interviewed live by the host of a popular weekly program called *Stories You Wouldn't Hear in the News*. A friend of a friend of the family knew him and had told him about this young kid, living in a middle-class suburb of Athens, who was strangely skilled at memorizing calendars. So he sought me out and brought me onto the program. Back then television in Greece was still quite primitive; everything was broadcast live (in black and white, of course) and absolutely nothing could be recorded or edited. I remember the host discussing this with my dad while the makeup crew were working on my face, asking if I would be able to perform my "tricks" under that kind of pressure, and I remember my dad reassuring him that nothing fazed me.

Two years earlier, when I was just four, my dad (who worked for Air Canada in Greece) had brought home one of those classic desktop airline calendars. That little triangular cardboard treasure instantly became my best friend. I loved all the black and red numbers, and once I figured out that the Sundays were marked in red, I began to try to make sense of all the patterns. (My mom had already taught me how to read and understand numbers because I was taking piano lessons.) Like all good airline calendars back then, this one spilled into the first two months of 1969, and I started to notice some interesting patterns: the same date in two different years was a different day of the week; and while in 1968 February had twenty-nine days, in 1969 it had only twenty-eight. I was completely mesmerized, kept asking questions and couldn't wait till the fall, when my dad finally brought home the brand-new calendar for 1969. Having both years in black and red in front me was like magic. I sat for hours learning the patterns and differences between the two years, and I began to memorize and compare the days in red: for instance, in April of 1969 the Sundays were the 6th, 13th, 20th and 27th, whereas in the same month the previous year the Sundays had been the 7th, 14th, 21st and 28th.

In my own primitive way, I had just learned how to tell what day of the week it would be (or had been) on any date, going back or forward as many years as I wanted. I didn't need any more triangular desktop calendars: all it took was memorizing fifty-two red numbers and learning when and how to add or subtract one or sometimes two days of the week to or from the previous year's calendar. None of it ever overwhelmed me; everything made sense. And of course I didn't understand why it was such a big deal for grown-ups or how I ended up in that TV studio. (Now I just wish they had made a recording of the show!)

Things only became more numerically interesting as I grew up. Numbers consumed me, talked to me, made more sense to me and more truly described the world for me than words. I relied on simple patterns to memorize count-less phone numbers, car licence plate numbers, weather statistics, track and field scores, car engine displacements and whatever else popped up in front of me. I reinvented Monopoly, much to my friends' frustration, by adding sales and income taxes, complex lending interest structures—anything that could satisfy my endless appetite for numer-ical stimulation. I aced math in school and I developed a massive weather-tracking project, which required that my parents buy me increasingly sophisticated thermometers, barometers and hydrometers so I could have more and more detailed figures to record, track and compare. When my parents moved homes a few years after I left for Canada, my mother accidentally tossed out a big box full of binders with all my weather stats—and I held a grudge for a very long time.

Once my brain was wired that way, it was impossible to unwire it, so numbers continued to follow me and talk to me right through my life. Time and basic social maturity gradu-ally helped me conceal some of my "numerosis," but digits and their relationships continued to dominate my brain all the time. Not surprisingly, I took an undergraduate degree in mathematics and computer science, and it was one of the easiest accomplishments of my life. My fascination with weather and climate gradually morphed into a much more serious study of climate change, which eventually formed the seed of my first social venture.

When my mother died, I noticed a tragic pattern of numbers. My mother's life and death were dominated, or perhaps almost predicted, by two digits (2 and 3) and their two single-digit products (6 and 9). Take a look at this:

- My mother was born in '39.
- She died in '99.
- She died on the 23rd day of the month.
- She died 36 days after her initial heart attack.
- She died 9 days after being discharged from hospital.
- My dad was 69 years old when she died.
- She was 60 years old.
- They had been married for 39 years.
- I was 36 years old.
- She was 23 years old when I was conceived.
- I was born on the 9th day of the month.
- I was born in '63.
- She was 26 when my brother was born.
- My brother was born on the 23rd day of the month.
- She died in my home, at 99 Harbour Square.
- My phone number at the time was 203-6666.
- My partner's phone number at the time was 932-9962.
- Both her parents had been born on the 3rd day of the month.

- My mother's mother died on the 9th day of the month.
- My mother's sister was born on the 9th day of the month.
- Both of my mother's siblings married people born on the 23rd day of the month.
- The sum of the digits of my mother's birthdate (27/02/39) is 23.
- The sum of the digits of her only sister's birthdate (09/09/41) is 23.
- The sum of the digits of her only brother's birthdate (18/01/49) is 23.
- (And, for some extra goosebumps, the *only* two other people I know whose birthdates add up to 23 are my partner, Joe, and my very special friend Summer Graham, who was born on one of the most numerically perfect dates: 23/06/93.)

That's how I've always seen the world. My accountants have always dreaded me. And all the kids in my life, big and small, run and hide when I start asking math questions.

NOTES

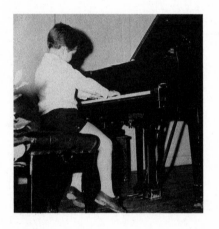

ONE OF MY DAD'S CHILDHOOD FRIENDS became a well-known musician and composer. His name is Mimis Plessas, and his fame and success in Greece spanned the second half of the twentieth century. Both he and my father were big lovers of jazz through their youth, and they were both gifted with excellent musical ears, but Mimis was the only one who trained in music and made a career out of it.

One day in early 1968, when I was four years old, we were at a restaurant with Mimis and his family. As was often the case, the grown-ups were egging me on by singing all sorts of well-known songs, and I kept singing along with them. I had been singing a lot since I was a toddler, and my dad was so proud of my apparent skill that he had been making reel-to-reel recordings of me since my first birthday. Mimis, impressed by the way I kept up with everyone's tunes, grabbed a carafe, poured varying amounts of water into a bunch of glasses on the table, handed me a spoon and then asked me to try to "play" a particular song by clinking the glasses. I took the spoon, tested each glass, rearranged them in the order of a full scale and started to play the song we had been singing a few moments earlier. Around the table, jaws dropped, and I remember Mimis leaning in to my dad's ear and whispering to him for quite a while. Then he got up, walked over to my side of the table, hugged me, looked into my eyes and said, "My little Andreas, you will become a big maestro someday."

Our two families began vacationing each summer in the same beautiful fortress town in southern Greece (more on this later), so Mimis and I would spend a lot of time together, going on boat rides, snorkelling, swimming, singing on the beach at night, talking about music and about the world. He was much more than my dad's old friend—he was my very own big, wise, fun, funny, sweet and caring life teacher and friend. I felt proud whenever I saw him on TV or heard him on the radio, and I remember marvelling at how perfectly he spoke not only his native Greek but also English. In those early years, he called me "maestro," and that made me feel pretty special. Later on he switched to calling me *glaraki mou* ("my little seagull"), because he had once helped me and my brother rescue and nurse an injured seagull.

That glass-clinking concerto changed my life. On Mimis's advice, my parents sought out one of the best-known piano teachers in Greece and plunged me into lessons at the ultra-tender age of four and a half. I couldn't read yet, so my mother had to quickly help me learn numbers (essential for reading notes and for hand positioning)—which was the real beginning of my love affair with those number-filled airline calendars. I was much smaller than any of the other kids I would sometimes see at my teacher's studio, and for many years I was too short to be able to reach the piano's pedals, so I had to learn to play and sustain sounds without them. But none of this made me feel strange: I just enjoyed all the attention and loved being able to use my fingers to create beautiful sounds from that big instrument. I didn't even mind all the pressure or the fact that within a couple of years I had reached a level where I had to practise piano for four long hours every day.

My teacher was the same well-known woman who had once taught piano to my mother. Her name was Katy Mavromichali, and she was a rotund, sophisticated, strict but gentle aristocrat from Istanbul and a descendant of a well-known Greek family of Constantinople from another time. I instantly became her favourite, and she heaped all sorts of attention on me. She made sure I was always her last student each Wednesday evening so she could have the freedom to stretch our time together, while my poor mom was left worrying about having to rush home with me so she could help my little brother with his homework.

Katy was incredibly demanding; I remember showing up at her studio each week and feeling the same intense anxiety, knowing she would make many critical comments and find all kinds of mistakes in whatever I had practised. Yet at the same time, she was warm and affectionate: she always had special sweet treats for me, always kissed me hello and good-bye, always asked questions about my school, my friends and our family vacation. She had no children of her own and, as the years wore on, she took to describing herself proudly as my surrogate mom.

Katy was well connected in the classical music community in Greece and knew how to push a kid to advance quickly in that world. My first public performance took place before

I had even turned seven. My first appearance on television was just a couple of years after that. My repertoire was exploding with each passing season, and I was soon competing against kids ten years older than me. My teacher confirmed early on what Mimis had discovered with those water glasses: I was gifted with what's known as perfect pitch—the ability not only to hear and understand the relationship between different musical notes but also to instantly and correctly name every note I heard, anywhere, anytime. Car horns, squeaking doors, chirping birds, airplane engines, phones, door chimes, human voices—all of those everyday sounds were instantly translated into notes in my head. Though I was unable to comprehend why other people couldn't do the same, I loved being able to impress and mesmerize grown-ups so effortlessly.

Yet somewhere deep inside me, the seeds of resistance and resentment were taking root. Four hours a day, every day (except Sundays), was a painful commitment for a youngster. I was expected to sit down at the piano at five o'clock each evening and, apart from short bathroom breaks, not leave the piano bench until nine. By that time, all that was left of my day was a quick dinner and bedtime. As the years passed, my friends would go out to movies or to the soccer field—while I was still working away at the piano. When I asked (and later started to protest) about it, the answer was always the same: "You have an incredible gift, and you can't possibly waste it. When you grow up, you will realize why it was important to work so hard and sacrifice so much at this stage in your life."

There were a few dramatic incidents along the way. I remember two in particular, with much sadness, as both involved my mother.

Because my dad travelled a lot, it fell to my poor mom to ensure that I never slacked off. Each evening, she was the one who watched and listened to make sure I didn't leave the piano bench for too long. Sometimes, if she had to leave the house for an errand, I would happily cheat and stay off the piano bench until the very last minute before she returned. But as long as she was in the house, even if she was napping (which was a standard afternoon custom for Greek adults back then), she was always on guard and there was zero wiggle room for me.

One afternoon, however, my grandparents showed up unexpectedly. I was very attached to them, and a visit like that was such a treat for me that, without even thinking about it, I stopped playing, sat on the edge of the piano bench and began to have a nice little chat with them while they waited for my mom to wake up from her nap. It never occurred to me, of course, that she was so conditioned to hearing me practise, even when she was asleep, that any but the shortest of interruptions would wake her up. All of a sudden, she burst into the living room in her nightgown—clearly without her contact lenses and unable to see much past her own nose. She rushed over to the piano bench, grabbed me by the ear, slapped me in the face a couple of times and yelled at me for being so irresponsible. The mayhem continued until her father jumped in to separate us. Only then did she pause, turn to him and say—I'll never forget this—"Oh my God, what are you doing here?" I felt angry and embarrassed, but also vindicated in an odd kind of way.

The second incident had to do with my sabotaging one of the strict rules imposed by Katy, my teacher. She was insistent that I never practise without a metronome unless I was at the final stage of learning a piece, when I had truly reached performance mode—the "colouring" stage, as she called it, when it was time to add some emotion and expression to all the technique I had learned. But until I got there, I was strictly forbidden to ever play so much as a single bar of music without a metronome. One day, budding troublemaker that I was, I shoved my metronome off the piano and onto the hard floor, making sure it was broken. Now I would not have to practise for the rest of that evening! Metronomes were not cheap, and certainly not in our family's budget, and the next morning my poor mom had to run all over Athens trying to find a new one. Not surprisingly, the new one didn't last long either; a couple of weeks later, it too "fell" off the edge of the piano. But that was the end of my runway to freedom. From then on, the third and final metronome stood on a low coffee table, over a soft carpet, and I never skipped practice again.

With the arrival of adolescence and the flood of hormones it brought, my resistance and resentment multiplied rapidly. I had peaked musically around the age of twelve or thirteen because, even though there was still plenty of room to grow, I was quickly losing interest and I could no longer be bothered to apply myself. My music books were filling up with Katy's angry red-ink notations and zeros for grades. I became more and more tuned out and miserable;

Katy became even angrier and more disappointed; but my parents desperately hung on to the hope that once I grew up a little more, I would rejoin the road to musical stardom. By the time I was fifteen, I had started negotiating reductions in the amount of time I was expected to spend practising, and four hours a day eventually dwindled down to two and a half hours. Even then, those 150 minutes each evening still seemed like torture. There was no escape. Each time I begged for permission to quit entirely, my parents' response was that as long as I lived under their roof, there was no other option: music was my life, and they would not let me throw away that gift. So I resigned myself to sitting hunched over the keys, all the while daydreaming about what life would be like the moment I finished high school and moved away to Canada. How amazing it would be to have all that "found" time each day!

And then things got even more complicated. As I began to plan my audacious move away from home and away from Greece and started to talk about going to the University of Manitoba for a science degree, my parents vetoed my decision. They were crushed by my rejection of their dreams for me. Just imagine: less than a half-dozen years earlier they had had a star kid on TV and in public recitals; they had spent every spare penny buying me the best piano lessons in town and the best books from overseas (not to mention replacing sabotaged metronomes); they had devoted so much of their own energy and time and passion over those fourteen years to help make it all happen—endless bus rides and taxi rides to the other end of town, just to make sure their gifted son got the best he could possibly get. They were living out an incredible dream of their own, and now here was their pimple-faced, angry teenager announcing that he never, ever wanted to have anything to do with music again. A stalemate ensued: they absolutely demanded that I continue with music, and I flatly refused.

Thankfully, a wise old friend of the family from Winnipeg, Lillian Cholakis, who became one of my earliest Canadian mentors, intervened with a brilliant compromise: she persuaded my parents to allow me to study whatever I wanted, as long as I went to a university with a strong musical culture where I could be indirectly influenced by those around me. The hope, of course, was that exposure to the right environment would somehow bring back to me the magic and the passion for music. And thus came about the plan to send me to Brandon University, two hours west of Winnipeg in the middle of the Canadian prairies, just so I could be immersed in a school that boasted the second-best conservatory in the country. I had no idea what fun and bizarre times I was setting myself up for (but that's a story for another chapter), so off to Brandon I went.

And then a funny thing happened: not long after I had left behind my home, my piano and my 150-minute daily torture sessions, I started to miss it all. After just a few weeks in Brandon, I found a piano room in the basement of my dorm building and began to book it so I could play there in the evenings. Then came the realization that I had something hot—word spread around campus that this new Greek kid was a really good pianist, and people started asking if they could come and listen when I played. I got a job at a local music school, teaching piano to gifted preschoolers. I was even hired to play the organ at the local junior league hockey games. And not long after graduating, as soon I could scrape together a thousand dollars, I bought myself a beat-up old upright. Then I bought a better one, and an even better one after that, and I'll never forget the day that my first baby grand arrived in my condo in Toronto. I felt as accomplished as those grown-up kids who buy their first Harley.

One evening in the summer of 1988, when I was visiting my parents back in Athens, they asked if I wanted to go to a wedding with them. It was taking place at the Astir Palace Hotel, a famous resort on a gorgeous peninsula at the southern end of the city, and the setting for the reception was incredible—all outdoors, under the stars, with a dreamy view across the bay towards the city. I sat at a separate table from my parents, and just as dinner was about to begin, the staff rushed to my table and started rearranging everything to create room for one more guest. The new spot was right next to me, and a few moments later the guest arrived. It turned out to be none other than Nana Mouskouri, Greece's biggest international diva of the 1960s, '70s and '80s. She had been living in Switzerland for many years, but was in Athens on vacation. Her husband had just flown back to Geneva, and she was spending a few extra days on her own at the resort. As is the custom when a celebrity is staying at the same venue where a wedding reception is taking place, she was formally invited by the newlyweds; but that was just the polite thing to do and they hadn't really expected her to attend. But apparently Ms. Mouskouri, who had never met the couple, had no better offers for that evening and decided to put in an appearance.

As if it wasn't bizarre enough that she ended up sitting next to me, I soon discovered that she knew my mother. They had met the previous week at the resort's swimming pool, where my mother went to swim every day, and had struck up a friendship. They were the same age and they spent a lot of their time talking about Canada, a country they both loved. Somewhere along the way they started to talk about me; my mother told Nana how excited she was that I was coming for a visit and, of course, she proudly told her all about my musical talent. So when she sat next to me and figured out whose son I was, she already knew plenty about me, and talk quickly turned to my music. I was pinching myself. Really?! Having dinner and drinks and laughs with Nana Mouskouri?! And she's interested in *me*?! The more wine she drank, the more I drank, and the more prepared we both became for the surprise that came next.

The band stopped playing and the lead singer announced that there was a musical celebrity among the guests: Would Nana like to join them on stage? Nana, who was several happy glasses of wine into the evening, strolled up to the stage, grabbed the mic, thanked the band and the guests for the warm intro and announced that she would sing *only* if her new young friend Andreas agreed to accompany her on the piano. Her new young friend Andreas instantly felt the same intense heat on his cheeks that he had felt twenty years earlier on that elementary school balcony, but obviously had no choice—the guests were already cheering—so he walked to the stage, sat on the piano bench in front of a few hundred strangers and set out on an unbelievable musical adventure.

We played, and improvised, and laughed, and got more and more into it—instead of just a couple of songs, we kept going (glasses of wine in hand, of course) under the stars until almost five in the morning. My repertoire seemed somewhat broader and more diverse than hers, and at one point I feared she might run out of lyrics (there were no iPhones back then!). This is when my overenthused father came to her rescue. He joined us on stage and whispered the lyrics of each new song into Nana's ear. It quickly turned into the Souvaliotis, Souvaliotis and Mouskouri comedy show, to endless laughter and applause from the audience. Somewhere along the way, in our scramble to come up with even more songs, I asked her if she knew anything by Billy Joel. She looked at me and said, "Wow. Billy. I haven't talked to him in so long. I wonder how he's doing." I was so pinching myself.

That was the start of a quirky friendship with Nana. After that, whenever she came to Toronto to do a concert, she would ask me how many friends I'd like to bring along—the first time, I was obnoxious enough to ask for sixteen tickets. We all went out for drinks with her after the concert, and my friends sat in disbelief as she chatted with them about their lives and signed records for their moms.

There have been all sorts of crazy musical encounters and adventures through the years. One of the most memorable was twenty years after the impromptu concert with Nana.

In the spring of 2008, I was in Sydney, Australia, for a conference, and a friend invited Joe and me to a private middle-of-the-night tour of the world's largest pipe organ, at the Sydney Opera House. My friend had paid some money to the man who had installed and was still maintaining that pipe organ just so he would let a few of us musicians and music lovers check out that majestic instrument when the venue was closed. We walked into the huge, dark opera house at midnight and climbed the tiny spiral staircase up to the organist's perch; then our tour guide switched the organ on, and we suddenly had the world's largest musical instrument, inside one of the most famous performance venues, literally at our fingertips. He encouraged us to try it, and of course once we got started we couldn't stop. I remember playing an endless stream of songs by the Beatles, Elton John and Billy Joel and even a selection of numbers from *The Phantom of the Opera* and marvelling at how that vast opera house reverberated. It was truly one of my life's peak experiences.

Through it all, however, it's still been tough wiping out the deep complexes and insecurities that piled up during those fourteen years of intense music training blended with prominence, social pressure and autism. To this day, I still have a hard time playing on command; it makes me feel used, and I come close to freezing up. I definitely play more easily if I've had a couple of drinks—and a lot better, according to Joe. It has taken a long time, but playing music is finally becoming just a beautiful hobby, nothing more than the distant echo of a complicated and defining phase in my early life. And with the passage of time it has become easier for me to feel more and to express myself more openly through my music.

When the original version of this book was translated into Greek and published in my birth country, it spawned a precious new friendship for me with a man called Robert Peck, who was then the Canadian ambassador in Greece. Robert was quite taken with my story and had arranged for the embassy to co-host the book launch in Athens. But he had also set up a remarkable surprise for me: the night before the launch event, which also happened to be St. Andreas's Day (name days are a big deal in Greece and are typically celebrated more than birthdays), he hosted a reception in my honour at the official residence. Among a small crowd of prominent members of Greece's arts community, he had also invited my original music mentor and glass-clinking concerto conductor, my dear old Mimis. After losing track of him across the Atlantic for decades, seeing him (as a hunched-over but exceptionally energetic and beaming ninety-year-old) at this event was an extraordinary thrill. We cried and hugged endlessly and entertained the other guests with fun stories about our unique and lopsided friendship—and then, naturally, we found ourselves glued to each other on Robert's piano bench. Our combo repertoire was eccentric, unpredictable, creative, multinational and utter fun—and my ability to share the bench and the keys with such a legend, without feeling any intimidation whatsoever, was shocking to me. I had finally grown up.

Mimis and I rekindled our special friendship that night, and I now often bend my travel plans so I can spend time with him. He seems unstoppable as he plays and composes his way towards his one hundredth birthday, and he continues to fill our world with gorgeous music and love. A few years ago, when I almost lost Joe to a complicated heart problem just weeks before our twenty-fifth anniversary, Mimis created yet another priceless gift for me: he composed, arranged and conducted the performance of several variations on a simple song I had written for my lover when we had first met, a quarter-century earlier. My incomparable grand old mentor asked me simply to play that piece on my piano in Toronto, record it on my phone and email it to him. Just a few weeks later he presented me with an absolute masterpiece, which, of course, I proudly presented to my recovering partner on our anniversary.

Speaking of beautiful circles in life, there is one more musical moment that I will never forget. My friend Rita called one Saturday morning to tell me that her dying mother had had a strange dream about me—she had dreamt that I was playing the third movement of Beethoven's *Pathétique* Sonata. No other musical project had consumed a larger slice of my childhood than mastering the *Pathétique*. When I was just eleven years old, it was a focus of my mother's love, my teacher's passion and my father's pride— and the absolute drain of all my energy. Ever since that time I had admired it from afar, hearing it occasionally on the radio and remembering every twist and turn, every painful transition and every impossible chord, but I just couldn't ever imagine going near it again. And all of a sudden, this sweet dying woman whom I hardly knew—and who had no idea I had ever played the piano, let alone the *Pathétique*—had mysteriously seen that story about me in one of the final dreams of her life. In an attempt to create an almost mirror image of the surprise Mimis had crafted for my ailing Joe a few years earlier, I quickly pulled out the sheet music, sat at my piano and managed my way through the first several bars of the third movement while Joe made a video of it. We rushed over to the palliative care hospice where we surprised Rita's mom with a real-life reproduction of her dream. She cried in disbelief, and then she was gone a few days later. But the mystery of her dream will stay with me forever.

ROOTS

I WAS THAT KID IN A HAPPY BUBBLE, the kid who (secretly) believed he was luckier than anyone else. And it was all because of how I saw my parents.

My dad, Yanni, had a massive influence on me. He was the smartest, wisest, sexiest, coolest, funniest, most worldly, most sophisticated and most popular dad. My teenage girlfriends fawned over him. Their moms (and all the other moms) were totally intimidated by him and engineered all sorts of creative arrangements so that they could catch a ride with him to parent-teacher days at our school. Our teachers were afraid of him. We were afraid of him. My mom was afraid of him. And yet we all adored him, followed him, quoted him, imitated him and craved his attention and approval. My dad was big, but his shadow was even bigger.

And yet, he really hadn't been born to be big. He was raised by a modest, shy, almost introverted father, a controlling mother and two older sisters in Greece's most miserable times during the Second World War. His childhood and adolescence were overwhelmed by the German occupation of Athens and the horrific Greek civil war that followed. He grew up hungry and scared, with no real plans for his future. He managed to finish high school but didn't study anything after that. He simply went into the army, as every young

Greek man was required to do, and then life just happened: he liaised with the Americans who were still operating military bases in Greece, improved his English and eventually found his way into the budding airline industry, first as a sales rep for British European Airways and eventually as the manager of Air Canada's sales office in Athens.

He lived at home until he married, at thirty, because that was really the only option he had. My grandmother was an exceptionally in-charge woman who ruled over her children's lives—in fact, her grip on them remained strong until the day she died, at almost a hundred. She was a special specimen of that final generation of Constantinople's Greek semi-aristocracy, most of whom were chased out of Istanbul by nationalist Turks after the First World War. As a young single woman, she found herself in unsophisticated Athens in the early 1920s and spent the rest of her life feeling, speaking and behaving a cut above those around her—including her own husband. She interviewed and tested her grandchildren's French-language nannies, entertained everyone with her singing and guitar playing at parties, terrified and terrorized us, cooked dreamy and exotic meals, had an opinion about everything and proudly ran the lives of her entire extended family. I remember as a teenager sitting at her dining room table, watching her examine my father's fingernails and lecture him about the way he cut them.

He lived safely under her apron until he married my mother—and spent most of the rest of his life balancing between the two very different estrogenic poles in his life. He had also been shaped significantly by his two older sisters.

The eldest, Toula, set the bar very high for the rest of the family. In the chaos and poverty of wartime Athens, she decided she would become a doctor, and began to chase her dream with single-minded determination. She specialized in anesthesiology, managed to become the first female anesthesiologist in all of Greece, married her successful and much older mentor, quickly amassed some serious wealth, became a widow at a young age, married another prominent doctor, built up even more wealth, and eventually, well into her seventies, retired from medicine and dove headfirst into her even bigger passion in life and was a famous playwright, poet and author in Greece well into her nineties.

My dad's other sister, Poppy, was a stunningly beautiful woman, sophisticated, kind, warm—the real soul of that family. My dad looked up to both of them and their controlling mother in genuine but complicated ways, and his personality, marriage and way of life were heavily influenced by these women.

Even though he had no formal education beyond high school, my dad had a scholar's depth of knowledge and the persona of a lecturer. He read and opined and debated all day long. There was no topic on which he didn't have a strong perspective: from economics to religion to politics to natural history to relationships to human sexuality, it was all his domain and he loved shaping his listeners' views. His job as an airline sales manager gave him two basic staples: a necessary income for his family and a semi-glamorous platform for his exploits and discoveries. He travelled as much as he could, so he could learn, meet, play, eat, drink and enjoy life to the max. For someone raised in such an intensely controlled environment, he had hit on the perfect career. Even as a married man with grown-up kids, he still regularly lied to his mother about when he was supposed to be back from each trip, just to give himself a bit more breathing room and avoid her phone calls on his first day back in town.

Although they had no financial headroom whatsoever, he and my mother would take advantage of every possible business trip to tour the world in fairly glamorous style on his employer's coin. Sometimes they would take us with them—and then we would instantly become the talk of our school, particularly in a country as poor as Greece in the 1970s, for jetting off to Rome or London or Vancouver a couple of times a year—but most of the time they would go off on their own. In the early years, in fact, when air travel was still a bit scary, they would travel separately and meet up in Hong Kong or Nairobi or Lima, so that if anything happened at least one of them would survive to take care of us.

But all that adventure and excitement still wasn't enough for my dad. His voracious mind needed deeper and more complex stimulation, so at a fairly young age he joined the Freemasons. The Freemasons became his cause and his passion, and he rose rapidly through their ranks. Eventually he blended his Greek nationalist passion with his Masonic philosophical appetite and became a prominent international representative and lecturer on behalf of the Freemasons of Greece. He thrived in that environment of constant debate, regular bouts of controversy, complex politics, and fame and recognition as an unlikely leader.

Growing up right at the core of a young, immature and unstable democracy also brought some interesting political threads into my dad's life. One of his two first cousins was a leading communist during Greece's civil war in the late 1940s and was eventually jailed and exiled. His other first cousin married a senior army officer who led the infamous 1967 military coup and became a senior participant in the notorious junta that ran Greece until the mid-1970s. He was convicted of all sorts of crimes after the junta was toppled and spent the rest of his life in prison. (He died on the day that I was writing this part of the book.) As if that wasn't enough political spice in one family, one of the best-known assassination victims of the past century in Greece was the brother of that famous old doctor who had mentored and married my aunt Toula; he was a popular, outspoken socialist in the early 1960s, and it was widely rumoured that the CIA was behind his murder in 1963, just a few months before I was born. (In fact, a popular American movie was made about his life and death, called Z—pronounced "zee"—which sounds like the Greek for "he lives.")

So that was my dad's world. It's what made him so complicated, wise, ambitious, scary at times, sexy in just about everyone's eyes and remarkably deep. He was also a very artistically talented guy, but had never enjoyed many opportunities to properly exploit those talents. He had an unbelievable musical ear, which, of course, made him my absolute terror whenever I practised piano near him. He was also a superb photographer and a sharp writer.

Not surprisingly, he spent his twenties dating countless women, many of whom ended up knowing each other, because his world in central Athens back then was tightly intertwined. Things never became particularly scandalous, but he always had lots of entertaining stories from that wild and playful era. And then, one day, he met my mother. She was barely twenty (he was almost thirty), had certainly lived a lot less than he had, but was confident enough to take him on. And within a year they were married.

My mom, Fofo, was artistic, but otherwise totally different from my dad. She was shy, and had been raised in a much milder, quieter, uncontroversial family. They had arrived in Athens only a few years earlier, as part of a mass exodus of foreigners from Egypt. Brits, Greeks, French and Italians had been the top colonizers of Egypt for generations and had enjoyed disproportionately comfortable lifestyles as the ruling class of that country. But the Egyptians began to stir after the Second World War, and the 1952 revolution was the beginning of the end for many of the resident minorities. Along with hundreds of thousands of other Greeks, my grandparents packed up the family and moved to Athens the following year. In a flash they went from being part of the ruling class to having to blend into a society that seemed to them a lot less refined than their foreigner "club" culture in Cairo. Egyptian Greeks spoke and lived differently than Athenians, and most of them formed their own cliques in their own separate suburbs of Athens. My grandfather continued to work for a Greek bank. My mom and her two younger siblings found it easier to adjust, and they soon thrived in their new hometown. The three kids grew in quite different directions. My aunt Haris became a well-known academic and architect specializing in Byzantine architecture, and together with her husband she spent most of her career restoring historic homes in the very special walled medieval "castle" of Monemvasia, in southern Greece. My uncle Nasos moved to England, became a marine engineer, married, had kids and stayed there for the rest of his life; he and I grew up almost as cousins, in fact, because he was so much younger than his sisters and closer to my age.

My mom finished high school and then started working an admin job at the American military base in Athens. That's where she met my dad. Their families got along right away, perhaps because of the expat connection, and the whole thing came together quickly. A month or two after the wedding, my dad got his first airline job and my parents began exploring the world. They waited four years before having children, mostly because they had the time and the appetite for fun and travel, but also because they didn't have any money. When I was born they were still living in a tiny apartment in the centre of Athens, which I think was costing them the equivalent of less than thirty dollars a month.

My brother, Nikitas, came along a year and a half after me. He was very different from me. He was smaller, to begin with, and he didn't really speak until he was three or four years old. He was a lot less social or expressive than most kids, and when he started to go to school, his special needs became much more apparent: he had trouble connecting with other kids, he required a lot of handholding just to keep up, and the teachers began to offer a range of suggestions to my parents about what was going on. The consensus was that my brother was developmentally delayed and that he should repeat one or two grades in order to properly catch up.

My poor parents, in the absence of any expert opinions, stubbornly began to fight back—because, despite my brother's social-skill challenges, they could tell he was actually a smart kid. So they were convinced that everyone else was wrong, and they persistently pushed him ahead. It took three more decades and a whole bunch of scientific progress before my brother's condition was finally diagnosed as being on the higher functioning end of the autism spectrum, so unfortunately, and like millions of other ASD kids around the world, he was raised with the expectation that he should live, learn, talk and adapt as if he was neuro-typical.

It was a rough and stressful ride, not only for Nikitas but also for the rest of us. My mother quit her job and dedicated much of her time to him. Both she and my dad armed themselves with the sharpest and most convincing arguments and stories about why their two sons were so different from each other; one was social (too social, perhaps), engaging and high-energy, while the other was shy, introverted and quirky, but both were presented as classic examples of how intelligence comes in multiple forms. Without realizing it, they were describing the great variety of personalities and styles of individuals on the autistic spectrum. Of course, in their passionate resistance to having their younger kid labelled "retarded," they stopped accepting expert advice on what may have been going on with my brother. It was perhaps not ideal, but nobody can ever blame parents for being protective and proud of their kids, particularly at a time when there was so little general knowledge about autism. The only unfortunate result of all that was the incredible pressure Nikitas had to endure all through his formative years—just because everyone's goal was to make him "normal."

Over time, my parents' relationship began to suffer under the pressure and strain of having to fight off society when it came to their kids' stark differences. My mom's domain was gradually reduced to just her home and a child who really needed her. My parents' trips together became less frequent and shorter. By the time she was forty, she had become increasingly dependent on alcohol (although it took the rest of us a lot longer to realize it), and my father had started to tune us all out in odd ways. They both became edgy and older than their age. There were still lots of beautiful family moments, and there was still plenty of real warmth and affection between the four of us, but the two of them were worn down and not particularly healthy. My mom smoked as well as drank heavily and began having mysterious blackout episodes, which we eventually realized were entirely linked to alcohol. I remember coming home from a high school party late one night and finding her standing in the kitchen, unable to speak or even understand anything I was saying to her. It was an awful realization for me and marked the start of her rapid decline.

By the time I was in my late twenties and my mother was turning fifty, both she and my dad were severely affected by her dependence on alcohol. She was a wreck physically, and he had become the classic angry, trapped and helpless spouse of an alcoholic. She frequently fell and hurt herself during her drinking binges at home, and he was so lost and desperate that he started to turn violent. Things were spiralling rapidly and dangerously until one day, after some ugly physical episode between them, she got into her car and disappeared. By the time my father worked up the courage to call me in Toronto and ask if, by any chance, she had shown up at my home, she had already been gone several days—and I remember my terror, imagining all the possibilities. To our enormous relief, she returned home soon after that—she had simply been cooling off at a hotel for a while, terrified of him and of her own demons. The first time we spoke after that, she announced to me that the two of them were "finished." I tried to sound cool about it and simply asked what would happen with their plans to visit me for Christmas, a few weeks later. She said she was still planning to come along with him but it would be a one-way trip for her—she wanted to stay with me after that and not return to Greece with her husband. I was mortified and confused but definitely not surprised.

The atmosphere was frigid when they showed up at my doorstep a few days before Christmas. Despite my mom's extreme volatility, her plan hadn't changed—she was still talking about leaving my dad and moving in with me. My dad's mood swings had become massive too—one moment he would try to sweet-talk her into forgiving him for having hit her and then he would abruptly lash out at both of us, her for everything she had done to him and me for being an enabler and a culprit by "stealing" her from him. She begged me to let her move into my condo and sleep on my sofa. I tried explaining to her how impractical a scenario that was. She persisted, tugging at heartstrings the way only a mother can. I felt so insanely trapped, almost to the point of panic. In the end, I came up with two conditions, and she agreed to both: she would stay with me temporarily until we found her a place of her own, and she would immediately enrol in a substance abuse program.

By the beginning of January 1993, my tormented and messed-up mother had become my roommate, my equally tormented and messed-up father had gone back home alone and was no longer speaking to me, and my neuro-atypical, barely twenty-nine-year-old soul was in chaos. The same mother who just a half-dozen years earlier had threatened to disown me for the way I was had now become a refugee on my sofa because of the way *she* was. My father was accusing me of choosing sides and was blaming me for wrecking their marriage.

Thankfully that was the lowest point; things quickly improved from there. I enrolled my mother in one of the best addiction management programs in town. I helped her get a basic job. We found her a tiny apartment, in the same building as mine. (I have the most tender memory of coming home from work and being able to go over to my mom's for dinner, something I had never experienced as an adult and had always envied among my friends.) My dad began to fly in from Greece every month, because he missed her so much. He would stay with her in her little flat, and they seemed to be enjoying a romantic renaissance. By the summer of '93, barely eight months into this upheaval, my mother announced that she felt confident, strong and clean enough to go back home, and off she went. The most intense, scary, destabilizing and transformative episode in our family journey was over in a flash. Sadly, my mom relapsed almost immediately and died within a few years.

Meanwhile my dad developed an exceptionally severe case of psoriasis, which he openly blamed on two things: the stress his wife caused him by choosing to be an alcoholic, and the embarrassment I caused him by choosing to be gay. His illness had a cascading effect on his overall health. His psoriasis was so debilitating that he ended up having to be put on a permanent chemo treatment, which, as the doctors had warned us, eventually wrecked his liver and killed him prematurely.

Strangely enough, all that intensity through my childhood years translated into positive energy for me. I felt lucky. I enjoyed the contrasts and the unique edges of our life as a family, even if I didn't yet understand what was lurking beneath. Who else could possibly have jet-setting intellectual parents, infamous political convict relatives from both extreme ends of the political spectrum and famous high-achiever family friends? That constant stimulation, positive as well as negative, was like being on an Adrenalin drip. It wasn't difficult to get hooked, and I grew up expecting more and more of it. Yet at the same time it was also easy to feel seriously at risk of becoming an underachiever. I thought I'd never grow up to be as big as my dad, as cool and edgy as my mom or as successful as some of the others around me.

Even my brother's extraordinary skills in certain areas— his photographic memory, for instance—would sometimes make me feel inadequate. Little did I realize back then that I was also growing up somewhere on that same spectrum, only with a different mix of skills and quirks. Decades later, when I finally learned about autism and about the countless possible shades and shapes it could take, the blend of my own unique skills, my social awkwardness and my unbearable pile of insecurities as an adolescent and a young man started to make a bit more sense.

SCHOOL

I SKIPPED KINDERGARTEN! I'm not sure why, and I never really asked. Maybe it had to do with my little brother's more obvious developmental challenges and my parents' anxiety about leaving him at home without his only sibling and friend for an entire year.

When it was time for me to go into Grade 1, I suddenly had a serious disadvantage compared with the other kids. I knew nothing about school or the social skills and routines that come with it. I was lost, and I fit in so poorly that after a couple of months, I had to be yanked out of the special school for gifted kids that my parents had worked so hard to get me admitted to. I remember feeling a bit embarrassed and confused by all that, but I'm sure it was much more painful for my parents. I transferred to a school closer to home and, after another couple of bumpy months, I finally settled in.

I thrived academically for twelve years, right till the end of high school. It was all so easy. The pace was too slow for me, and I could easily have become bored and difficult; thankfully, I was kept busy and challenged with my much more intense piano life.

My inadequate or abnormal social skills made me a remarkably unfiltered and unedited keener: front row, hand up in the air all the time, eager to impress, but also scared of all the teasing I was sure to get from the cool kids. I knew I was different, but most of the world was telling me that was okay, that I was different in a good way.

I learned to skim the tips of waves at school so efficiently that I became academically lazy. I didn't have much choice, considering how little time I had for homework—as soon as I got home each day, I'd have to start on my four hours of piano. I rarely crammed and always did well, but I was certainly not developing any proper discipline. I knew I had become the ultimate optimizer, and I bragged about it.

I was also becoming an optimizer on a different level: because of my social awkwardness, but also because I had been spoiled by my ability to maximize my returns with minimum effort on the school front, I began to gravitate away from social situations that would stretch or challenge me. I didn't hang out with the other smart kids in my class, because I couldn't be bothered to work as hard to keep up with them as friends. I wanted lots of friends, and my measure of success was definitely the size of my herd, but it was all about optimizing the quantity, not the quality or depth, of relationships. So I started to hang out with kids who weren't quite at the top of our class, like I was, or those who were younger than me, including all my younger cousins. It took my parents a while to clue in; at first they just thought their son was such a generous soul, being friends with everyone and acting as a bit of a shepherd to the younger ones. But eventually they noticed the real pattern and worked hard—unsuccessfully—to change me. My mom used to mock me and call me "king of the little people." She used to tell me

I would never learn anything that way, but that didn't faze me, perhaps because that's all I could handle. None of us realized it back then, but I think I was already operating at the absolute limit of my social capabilities.

Other interesting symptoms of my underdeveloped—or weirdly developed—social filters involved trust and sharing. In my eagerness to belong and to be appreciated, I wouldn't pause and measure anyone or anything, as most kids do: I would dive right in, throw myself wholesale into a social situation and hope that my generosity would earn me something. And this wasn't just when I was a little kid; this was my MO right through adolescence. No filters at all. If I liked you and wanted you in my life, I would immediately throw everything I had at you, from family secrets to invitations to spend the entire summer with us. I would come home and tell my mom I had promised my new friend Yanni that she would drive him to his German lessons. It was a constant fiesta of unfiltered trust and largesse, which just drove my parents crazy—and their expanding paranoia about it drove *me* crazy with fear and insecurities.

By the time I went to university, I had so mastered my optimizer skills that I breezed through my undergraduate degree. I could even optimize the effort in advance, because I now had the option of choosing the courses that I knew I could easily ace. (In high schools in Greece back then, there were no electives whatsoever.) And on the social front, there was a great new twist to the previous "king of the little people" mode: king of the vanilla people! In Brandon, Manitoba, the exact centre of the whitest and most homogeneous part of the country, I stood out like that single tree in the middle of the flat prairie. I didn't have to be cooler or more socially sharp—I just had to be me, with my weird accent, my funny name, my crazy stories about my faraway birth country. Without any effort and without needing to find a bunch of "little people," I was king again. It was an even easier ride this time.

I had grown up enough to know what I was doing and why I was doing it. All those childhood lectures from my parents about avoiding the easy road meant I had nagging doubts about the superficiality of my reign and whether I was in fact learning or gaining much this way, but I was unstoppable. And, on reflection, I think I still learned plenty. I may have been clawing to the top of my social heap in unusual or unorthodox ways, but I was still succeeding— and I was learning exactly how to spot my niches and how to harness them.

GAY

I REMEMBER THE FIRST TIME my dad said it. Then he said it again a few weeks later. And he kept saying it, in one form or another, for many years. It was that horrible line about how it would be easier for him if one of his sons died than to find out he had a "faggot" son.

I remember my heart pounding in my chest each time I heard him say it. I remember the panic and the desperate hope that swirled in my head that somehow I had it all wrong, that somehow this attraction I had always felt towards other boys was something that would eventually go away. I *had* to be wrong about it—because otherwise life seemed like an impossible dead end. I was utterly terrified of what was in me.

People always ask me how old I was when I first knew, and they expect to hear one of the typical responses from a gay man of my era: fifteen, seventeen, maybe even twenty years old. My answer is different: six, seven or at most eight years old. I was a tiny, geeky, "gifted" kid when I first heard my dad say those ghastly words—and that's all it took. I knew instantly. I knew it with as much certainty as I do today. All it took for it to come to the conscious surface was that terrifying statement by my awe-inspiring father. It was the most crushing, revelatory moment of my life. I was done. I was worthless. And this was when I was in Grade 2 or 3.

Greece in the 1970s was definitely a frightening place to be growing up gay; my dad was just an ordinary, progressive man in that time and place. He was no more homophobic than his buddies or than a lot of my friends in school later on, but he was my god, the best and most intimidating communicator, and I had never doubted anything he said. So when that line first came out of his mouth, it felt like the end of the world for me.

Looking back, I think that this moment may have been one of the most useful turning points in my life. That realization of being different, of being alone, of having to compensate for what I thought was going to be a massive handicap, of having to manage and cover up and navigate around my nature—all of that quickly morphed into incredible strength and skill. It was no different than what happens to those scrappy little kids who grow up on the street: they may be afraid at first, but they end up developing layers of confidence and survival skills.

So there I was, growing up with this enormous—and enormously premature—secret. There were traps and scares everywhere, and I had to constantly manage. I worked hard to change my "feminine" handwriting, to hide or eliminate all my expressive hand gestures on the piano, to speak differently, to play rough, like all the other boys in school. It was all conscious effort, all the time. And every time my dad would utter some variation of that line, I would work even harder at it—and I would panic, thinking that maybe he was saying those things because he was on to me.

I had a gay great-uncle and a gay teacher. They were both

warm and caring, and my parents seemed to have pleasant relationships with them, but that didn't make me feel any better. They were grown-ups, I reasoned, so whatever respect they got must have been because of that; as a kid, I must have been worth nothing. Plus, even though my parents connected with them and allowed them into our lives, they would still make all sorts of demeaning references and jokes about them behind their backs.

By adolescence, the hormones were overflowing, the fantasies were overwhelming, and the guilt was almost unbearable. As a ten-year-old, I had felt frightened because I knew I liked boys. As a fourteen-year-old, I felt trapped and terrified because I couldn't stop thinking about boys. I was ready to do something about it, no matter how huge the risk, and the only reason I didn't was because I couldn't quite figure out how or with whom. As confident as I may have been by this point in my own sexuality, I still felt like an extreme aberration, and I thought that finding someone else like me would be next to impossible.

And then came my friend Makis. He and his family had just moved to our part of town, so he showed up in our school at the start of Grade 10. He and I hit it off right away—cool kid, smart, sensitive and good-looking. Also, our fathers knew each other because they were both Masons, which immediately became our special secret, because the Masons were broadly vilified by the Greek church and functioned like a secret society. I latched on to that extra hidden bond between us and kept building on it from there. In no time, this had turned into my first real infatuation, and

Makis kept feeding it more and more fuel by being so friendly and close to me—but without having the slightest clue about my emotions. We were hanging out all the time, chatting on the phone for hours, studying together and spending weekends away at friends' cottages. And the pain and the hunger kept growing until I couldn't live with it anymore. Even though I knew there was almost no chance any of what I felt was mutual, I decided it was time to break my silence.

I remember the moment as if it were yesterday. We were at his place and I asked him to go for a walk with me so we could talk about something serious. (I was too scared to have that conversation under his parents' roof.) As soon as we were a couple of blocks from his home, I stopped, looked him in the eye and said simply, "I really wanted you to know that I'm gay."

I felt as if I had just pushed myself off the edge of the highest diving board in the world. I said it quickly, without hesitation, but as soon as the words were out of my mouth, I felt as if I was twirling and tumbling through the air. But it was too late to shift my gaze, and so, with the sun hot on my face, I kept looking straight at him. Makis locked eyes with me and, his voice calm, said, "Good for you, for trusting me with this. I am your friend."

So there it was: that earth-shattering first coming-out moment in a man's life. Except I wasn't a man—I was barely fifteen. The hormonally charged side of my brain might have been hoping for a different outcome from that exchange, but I couldn't have gotten anything better from

Makis. He wasn't gay, he wasn't interested in me that way, but he was my friend—and he was cool with how I was. His simple response taught me immeasurably much about life and the world that lay ahead: real and balanced friendships, the beauty of genuine revelations, the wondrous intertwining of trust and vulnerability in human relationships, the value of communicating and sharing confidently. All I was trying to do was express, and maybe even satisfy, my desperate hidden passion, but instead I got a fantastic lesson on deep human relationships. This was the defining moment of my adolescent years.

Makis and I drifted apart over time. After high school we both moved to different corners of the planet and lost touch. It was only in our late forties, through Facebook, that we found each other again and I discovered that he lived just a short drive away from our godchildren, on the east coast of Australia. It didn't take me long to engineer a visit—and I felt blessed when, with that bit of extra confidence that thirty years of adulthood had given me, I was able to raise a glass to him in his own home, in front of his very proud wife, and thank him for that world-changing response to me a whole lifetime earlier.

The rest of my adolescence was uneventful but still very troubling. I was alone. I was too driven and too hungry for life, and I couldn't just resign myself to being alone. So I began to think about moving to Canada. A few years earlier, Air Canada had come close to transferring my dad to Edmonton, and in expectation of that, they had rushed our family through the immigration process. In the end, the transfer never happened, but we were left with fully approved immigration visas—and the option of moving to Canada, either as a family or as individuals. I already liked Canada; apart from its wacky climate, which was a feast for my weather-obsessed mind, it felt like a good, fair, open, energetic and youthful society. In so many ways it provided the perfect fix for all my frustrations with Greek society, and it also offered me one other very simple advantage—distance!

My parents didn't object. They too liked Canada and saw plenty of opportunity for their young, ambitious son (without having a clue about what was really pushing him away). The distance didn't bother them—they would be able to fly over to see me as often as they wanted at no cost—and they jumped on board and helped me plan my big move for the summer of 1981, right at the end of Grade 12.

And off I went: fearless, restless, reckless, tireless and filled to the brim with energy to explore, to live and to build. It was an unbelievable high. It didn't matter to me where I was; I was just happy to have been unleashed onto the world, and I couldn't get enough of it. I showed up in tiny Brandon, Manitoba, and created my own little hurricane in that town. I met all the local Greeks and persuaded them to start a Greek school for their kids. I started and anchored—with my new big Afro hairdo—a weekly Greek TV news program on the community channel. I got a job teaching piano to kids. And I acquired an army of new friends as well as a few boyfriends and girlfriends among them. The repressed and trapped suburban kid from Athens was making up for lost time in so many ways.

I remember thinking that it was perfectly normal and safe to be dating both a local girl and a local boy at the same time—one was fulfilling my social "fitting-in" needs and the other was fulfilling everything else. But big-city boy from Greece miscalculated the odds of connections in a small prairie town. When I went back to Greece for the summer I started sending them identical postcards with identical messages ("I love you, I miss you, see you in September"). The girl happened to be the boy's best friend, and because the boy was deep in the closet, my relationship with him had been hidden from her, and our paths had never crossed. He naturally hid his postcards, but she proudly displayed hers in her apartment—and it didn't take long for him to spot one and figure it all out. Mayhem ensued. When I returned to Brandon in September, I found the two of them standing together in front of my dorm room, ready to have a very interesting conversation with me.

The carnage from those first few years in Brandon was considerable, but so were the memories and the beautiful growing up that came with it.

Through those early, unleashed years, I stopped worrying about what my parents thought or didn't think about the way I lived. I never wanted them to know, but I had also become a bit more careless, courtesy of the great physical distance that now separated us. I would easily and creatively put my life on hold each time they came to visit, and I became good about building the right safeguards during my playful summers in Greece. I thought that they considered their hyper kid a heterosexual Casanova, but this was naive thinking on my part. Slowly, very slowly, my tiny slip-ups, my mysterious patterns, my colourful friends and everything else in my whirling life synthesized into a pattern of suspicions in my parents' minds. And then came the big blow.

It was the seventh of October, 1985. I had already graduated and was living in Winnipeg with my brother and working at my first job, as a computer programmer. After a short visit with us, our dad was about to fly back to Greece. It had been a bit of an awkward few days: he had made some uncomfortable comments about my "faggy" friends and my weird clothes and slightly radical hairdo. With my thickened skin and life-devouring brain, I hadn't been too concerned about the things he said. I kissed him goodbye that morning and went off to work. A couple of hours later, he called to ask if he could borrow one of my small suitcases because he had run out of space in his own luggage. "Sure," I told him. "Go into my bedroom and take my blue Samsonite from the closet." And that was it. In those few seconds, with a special twist of irony that involved my closet, years and years of elaborate schemes and firewalls came crashing down. I had just unleashed the biggest scare in my young life and the biggest implosion in my relationship with my parents.

Inside the suitcase, he found a revealing letter I had written to a boy I had planned to visit back in Brandon months before. The visit had been cancelled, the letter had never been delivered, and I had completely forgotten about it still being in that suitcase. I was done. I was suddenly faced with the evolved version of my dad's horrible threat from my childhood years. It was no longer about preferring to have a dead child instead of a gay one. Now, with the choice already made for him, it was simply about his not wanting to be alive anymore. When he called me at work after he had read the letter, all he could say to me was that his life was finished and that I might never hear his voice again. Sobbing, he kept asking how I could do this to them and assured me the news would undoubtedly kill my mother too. He said he hoped the plane taking him to Greece would crash, so he wouldn't have to ever face her again and break her heart by telling her about his horrible discovery.

I sat at the other end of the phone shivering, feeling as if my world had abruptly ended. That was one of only two moments in my life when I felt numb and paralyzed by shock. (The other was just a few years later, when I happened to witness the public beheading of a convict in Saudi Arabia.) I spent the rest of the day alone, terrified and with absolutely no survival plan.

And then the phone rang, early the next morning. My mom was calling from Athens to let me know that my father had arrived, had shared the news with her and that she was packing her bags and flying out right away to be with me. She sounded upset but not angry, and promised me that everything would be all right and that we would work together to "fix" the problem; she was already making arrangements for me to see someone about it. My paralysis was at once replaced with smiles and hope and excitement.

That she was still speaking to me—heck, the fact that they were alive and making plans—felt like a huge gift, compared with how life had seemed when I went to bed the night before. I may have been cocky and hungry and restless and fun-seeking all these years, but I was still a scared little kid with the self-confidence of an average twenty-two-year-old, so I was ready to embrace any plan that could perhaps "fix" my biggest handicap in life. When my mom showed up in Winnipeg the next day and told me I was scheduled to see one of the best-known psychiatrists in town, I was on cloud nine—not in a logical kind of way, but just because. In that kind of extreme crisis mode, any escape path would do.

And so I went to see that psychiatrist and I remember being fascinated by how calm he was; the contrast between the two of us must have seemed hilarious to him. He opened by asking me why I was there. "Because I'm gay," I replied. His next question was whether it had been my own decision to come to see him or if someone had sent me. As soon as I told him it was my parents who had arranged it, he closed his notebook, looked me straight in the eye and said (I'll never forget this), "All right, then, we're done. It's your parents who need to come and see me, not you. Thanks for taking the time, and thanks for answering my question honestly."

I reacted with a weird mix of emotions. Was it a letdown? Had I been hoping that a pro might have some magical solution for my "problem"? Was I just craving a friendly listener, someone who could untangle the unimaginably raw emotions I'd been experiencing for the previous few days? Or was I simply feeling vindicated? I drove home, shared the news with my anxious mom and then watched her implode. She pounded her fist on the kitchen counter, cried, swore and talked about how those "quacks" were all the same. She never went to see my new favourite quack, but that moment marked the beginning of a very slow, often volatile, almost always painful but unbelievably important maturing in our relationship. The scrappy little kid had just inadvertently reached the summit of another huge mountain and was now finally ready to live an honest life.

It's amazing how much less complicated and tiring life becomes when you stop having to manage firewalls and personas. Most gay men and women of my generation developed quirky or complicated edges precisely because they were made to feel so different and, in most cases, so much lesser than the rest of the population. They had to compartmentalize their lives and stories and affections. But once you remove that need to behave differently, once you allow people to live open and honest lives like everyone else, then suddenly you find them growing up and living with far fewer fears and complexes. I so wish that someday all gay kids will be able to grow up feeling as normal and as honestly integrated in society as I began to feel after that big and accidental revelation at the age of twenty-two. And I think that, in Canada at least, we're well on our way.

My life after October 1985 was so much simpler and more authentic compared with my life before. It became about living, about absorbing and experiencing and sharing and loving, instead of managing, separating and packaging. My lifestyle could finally match my personality: I could dive, instead of hesitating and calculating; I could love, instead of being afraid; I could celebrate, instead of pretending. That scary moment of revelation was almost like a second birth.

It took a long time for things to become truly comfortable with my parents, but I found the work-in-progress mode of our relationship quite stimulating. I didn't mind or fear their unpleasant comments anymore; I just saw an interesting challenge and sometimes entertained myself by trying to use a bit of shock therapy to shift their perceptions. When they were apart, they would each try to accommodate and understand and adapt a lot more, but as a pair they were more difficult and at times militant, perhaps because they habitually reinforced and supported each other's homophobic tendencies. I was fascinated that they had abruptly inherited my previous need for secrecy and compartmentalization. Now that they were in on the big secret, they treated it as their own—and they spent the rest of their years managing perceptions, questions, stories and assumptions among all their friends and relatives. Having been there in very painful ways through my formative years, I understood their pain, and out of respect, I didn't interfere. Because of that, some of my closest and dearest relatives didn't really know much about my life and didn't even get to know or love my Joe until after both my parents were gone. Once again, I know that those who come after us will have it a lot better and easier.

I drew a huge amount of energy and inspiration from my newfound openness. In fact, I enjoyed becoming a bit of an early role model. When I got my first senior executive job, in the mid-1990s, I felt uniquely proud to be an openly gay leader in a fairly large organization—and I enjoyed having the disproportionate ability to help boost the confidence of some of our younger gay employees and support the perception shift of others.

A decade later, when I was chasing my first CEO job, I spent a day with an industrial psychologist as part of an in-depth assessment, and I didn't hesitate to reveal that I had a same-sex spouse (and that escaping the homophobia of my country of origin had been my main reason for immigrating to Canada years earlier). The psychologist didn't look at all surprised or uncomfortable, and I certainly ended up getting the job. A month or two later, he invited me out to lunch and shared two things with me. First, he told me how surprised he had been by my revelation, because in all his years of assessing or coaching organizational leaders he had almost never come across another openly gay CEO. Second, he said that he too was gay. Interestingly, he shared this with me in confidence. We went on to become close friends, and the two of us now share a mission to inject and inspire even more of that kind of openness into the corporate world. But I was still fascinated (and perhaps, secretly, a bit excited) by the fact that I had been on one of the bleeding edges of our society's evolution.

Shortly after that, I was invited to join the Young Presidents' Organization (YPO), the largest global association of CEOs, a club that is viewed by many as being a bit testoster-one-heavy. I hesitated (for once!). I remember grilling the then chair of the Toronto chapter, where I was being recruited, about that perception and about how a gay member could fit in. He responded with enthusiasm about how good it would be for the chapter finally to have someone like me and about how cool and progressive I would find the whole organization. And so I dove in, becoming the first openly gay member not only in Toronto but in all of Canada—more than a thousand CEOs across the entire country and not one openly gay man or woman until I showed up. It was interesting how quickly that tiny aspect of my DNA turned into a serious personal edge in an organization that is so sharply focused on progressive leadership. Joe and I—we'd been immersed in YPO together from the start—suddenly found a perch from which we could really make a difference by naturally influencing some of the sharpest and most prominent leaders in our country. We didn't have to say or do anything differently; by simply being who we are we imperceptibly guided our fellow members (and, just as importantly, their kids) through the beautiful notions of inclusion, acceptance and the genuine harnessing of our differences.

UNFILTERED

THE DESERT OCTOBER SUN felt extra hot on my face as I sat at the edge of a giant resort swimming pool in Las Vegas, looking down at my little brother, who stood chest-deep in the water in front me. He was mostly listening and I, more nervously than ever, kept talking, explaining, analyzing, dredging up examples and life stories. Nikitas was definitely my "little" brother at that moment, even though he was already forty-two years old. And I was hyperconscious of how that particular conversation was the most significant, most delicate and, as it turns out, most impactful one of our lives as brothers.

Years earlier, a young cousin of ours in Greece had decided to focus her speech therapy work on autistic children. It didn't take her long to spot the striking similarities between her young clients and her older cousin Nikitas. Fascinated, she asked me if my little brother's obvious autism had ever been formally diagnosed. Without intending it, she triggered the gradual demolition of that extra-thick wall of silence and denial that our proud parents had so carefully erected and guarded over a lifetime.

My mother had already died by this point and my father was the sole remaining custodian of their fiercely protected pride. In my own autistic, unfiltered way, oblivious to the web of tender emotional strings I was about to start unravelling and shredding, I sat my dad down and, naively full of enthusiasm, tried to share the revelation as a good-news story. We finally knew why Nikitas is the way he is—isn't that clarity and confidence wonderful? Isn't it great to understand his strengths and limitations so much better, to be able to maximize opportunities and minimize challenges and threats for him? I was full of pride for helping lift the lid off a crippling family mystery.

The only form of violence missing from my father's reaction was physical. He thundered like never before, and the shockwaves reached far and kept reverberating right up until the moment of his death. In his eyes this was the most extreme violation of his private world, an audacious, pointless and indictable dismantling of his life's most precious, most sacred and fiercely guarded project. His younger son was perfectly "normal," and anyone who suggested otherwise was nothing but a nasty gossiper. He immediately stopped speaking to the shameless culprit cousin. He threatened to do the same with me unless I put a permanent lid on that pathetic topic. And he ended up leaving this world a couple of years later fully convinced and terrified that his honour would be tarnished posthumously by the ridiculous, baseless chatter about him having raised an autistic son. If only he'd known—if only *I* had!—that the final count of autistic sons he raised would turn out to be greater than one.

I remember a Saturday morning in the fall of 2007, when I was huddling in a coffee shop with my friend Guy, inhaling his precious advice about how to open up to my little brother on our trip to Vegas the following week. Guy was the brilliant industrial psychologist who had assessed me for my first CEO job a couple of years earlier—it was our coming out to each other that triggered the start of our special friendship. He knew all about my brother and the impossibility of talking to him (or even about him) while my father was still alive, but now my dad was gone and I was presented with an opportunity to go on a bonding trip with my little brother. Guy felt strongly that Nikitas would live more happily, much more happily, if he understood his condition and how it affected his daily life. He coached me so carefully on how to engage my brother in that conversation, how to talk to him about autism, about special skills, limitations, behavioural guardrails, opportunities and changing attitudes. And I remember leaving that meeting full of excitement, gratitude and nervousness.

Nikitas had never travelled alone. His holidays had been limited to either visiting our parents in Greece, where he felt appropriately looked after and comfortable, or sometimes travelling with them. He later shared with me that he felt under a lot of pressure when he was with them, particularly as he grew older and craved more independence, but he felt he had no options.

And then our parents were both gone and my little brother was left without his natural support system. As soon as our father passed away, Nikitas attached himself much more meaningfully to me and Joe—it was obvious he needed sounding boards and sources of advice, and we were clearly required to fill the gap. But he also needed to figure out what to do about his vacations. Would he now have to learn to travel on his own and would that be easier and less stressful for him than having to depend on us? In the first year after we were "orphaned," he tagged along with us and a few of our friends on a fun trip to Greece and he definitely enjoyed himself, but that wasn't something we could repeat for him every year.

So in 2007, when I was extra busy building my first venture and couldn't manage to escape town for more than a few days, Joe and I found ourselves helping him make his own travel plans for the first time. He wanted to return to Las Vegas. He had been there before with our dad, had loved the enormous hotel swimming pools, and, of course, his condition made familiar places and experiences much more appealing. I helped him book his flights and a room at the same resort as before. Then, just when I thought we were all done, came the most touching request I have ever gotten from my wonderful little brother: he called and asked if I would consider joining him on the trip, at least for the first couple of days, just to help him settle in. I hesitated, because I had never imagined him asking for such a thing, and also because I was so absorbed by the intensity of my work. But Joe, who is normally so much less decisive and outspoken, immediately pointed out that I had no choice: I had to go! This was such a tender, vulnerable admission by my little brother that he needed my support. It would be so simple and so easy for me to make a huge difference, just by helping ease him into living more independently in the future.

So here we were, under the hot Vegas sun, symbolically arranged in a bit of a lecturer/student angle, with me sitting on the edge of the pool deck and him standing in the water below me, both of us awkwardly managing a bit of staccato eye contact. I opened up with an uncomfortable "I wanted to talk to you about you" line. He seemed surprised but curious. I then asked if he understood that he's different from most people. Instantly the tension skyrocketed—he responded with a curt "yes." My heart was now pounding. Next question: "Would you like me to talk to you about how you're different?" This triggered another affirmative one-word response and an even more intense sunburn feeling on my cheeks. And then came the snowball: as soon as I started to describe autism, he became so engaged—suddenly there was a lot more eye contact, a lot more back-and-forth, clarifying questions and a torrent of comments. He seemed so curious about, and so genuinely surprised by, the news. It was obvious that, in the absence of any formal diagnosis or even any conversation in the past about his differences, he had come to his own conclusions. Sadly, but perhaps naturally, he had interpreted all the signals he had ever received as evidence that he was developmentally disabled. And now, the myth was being demolished before his eyes—I could see those eyes filling with relief. He was opening up more and more to me, hungrily asking more questions and starting to smile. He was smiling! He was trusting and loving the revelation. And my proud big-brother heart was melting. At some point, he looked up at me and said: "Is me being autistic just as normal as you being gay?"—and that instantly became the most defining moment of our life as siblings. Here was my pure, smart and tormented little brother, revealing how abnormal and marginalized he had always felt, but also inadvertently reassuring me that our parents' homophobia and lifelong disapproval of me had not spilled over to him. He was pronouncing the word "gay" to me for the first time ever, in his own beautiful way celebrating our individual differences and our own special ways of fitting into this world.

His life was never the same after that Vegas trip. He flew home confident, curious and so much better prepared for an independent life. His communication style gradually morphed and he became much more self-aware. He learned to anticipate uncomfortable moments and settings; he started to speak openly to us about his limitations and to brag about his extraordinary skills. As a young retiree now, he travels the world fearlessly and enjoys pushing his boundaries, little by little.

The other life that was changed fundamentally was mine. Besides the deep gratification that came from that special sharing experience, the much bigger treat for me was the transformative discovery that came with it. Nikitas wasn't the only autistic one in our family. Everything Joe and I had read about my brother's condition had revealed to us, without any doubt, that I also belonged to a spot some-where along the autistic spectrum. I may have been higher functioning than my little brother, I may have masked things and expressed myself differently, and my coping mechanisms may have been more developed, but I was far from neuro-typical. My formal diagnosis came much later, partly necessitated by the writing of this book, but to us it had all become extremely clear as soon as we began to learn about autism—and my psychologist friend Guy also contributed a great deal of clarity about it.

All my quirks, my barely controlled social awkwardness, my extraordinary math and music skills, my chronic and frustrating discomfort with eye contact, my obsessive love of order and routine, my trouble coping with disruptions and unexpected events—all of it now started to make sense. Just like my little brother, I had spent a lifetime trying to mask or minimize all those things, trying to be just like everyone else—but I simply couldn't be. When we finally figured it out, it made an enormous difference having a spouse who had always loved the raw and real me. I think if I'd gone through this type of self-discovery alone, I may have taken a bit of a confidence hit, not knowing how the world would accept me as an officially "different" person. Joe and I went through the revelation journey together, as we read books by autistics or about autism, and he wasn't surprised or concerned by any of it. He had always loved everything that stood out about me, annoying or not, and it was in fact helpful for him, too, to be to able to wrap a well-understood label around it all.

The longer I processed the revelation, the more it added to my sense of relief and self-confidence. I had always lived with the deepest insecurities about every weird corner of my strangely wired mind, and I always tried so hard to mask

my differences. When I was a kid, my parents would sometimes come into my room while I slept and mess up the
order of the pens and books on my desk, just to make fun of
my obsessive tendency to stack and line things precisely and
consistently. I would then try hard to pretend I hadn't noticed
and hadn't been upset by their trick—even though I would
be anxious about it as soon as I realized what they'd done
and couldn't even visit the bathroom before painstakingly
returning everything to its only acceptable position. When
my spouse or friends joked about my "unfiltered" personality
and my inability to nuance or cushion my exchanges with
people around me, I would respond defensively or even
angrily but would always feel embarrassed about the way
I was perceived. I was desperate to find a way to change my
style—but nothing would change, of course, because nothing *could* change.

My career was definitely affected, in so many ways. Some
of my autistic traits undoubtedly contributed to my intensely
entrepreneurial style and aptitude, my unquashable hunger
to always build or disrupt, and my pure intellect. But the
flip side of all that was so often painful, debilitating and
alienating. I couldn't ever fake anything (Joe always jokes
about my uncontrollably disrespectful body language when
I am onstage with other speakers who are boring me); I suffer in chaotic or disorganized situations; I really struggle to
read faces; and I miss so many more social cues than the
average person.

By the time I launched Carrot, I was completely out
about my autism and found the shared awareness incredibly

helpful in so many ways. Even when my behaviour or my body language was edgy, it caused far fewer issues with employees than it had before, because it was now so much easier for everyone to understand me and even to anticipate my reactions. We built wonderful counterbalancing structures inside our company that allowed me to thrive in my own extraordinary ways without my needing to normalize myself. I felt so at home, so much more empowered to think, speak and change things my way—and I am absolutely confident there was plenty of correlation between our success and our openness in that respect.

FOREIGNER

MY DAD AND I were riding the busy elevator up to my tenth-floor dorm room in Brandon when he started to say something to me. I panicked. He was speaking in Greek, and all the other students in the elevator could hear him. It was so embarrassing. I tried to shut down the exchange by acknowledging him with just simple sounds, not even words. I kept staring at the floor. And he kept talking.

There were so many similar scenes with my visiting parents during my early years in Canada—all of them equally embarrassing to me. I couldn't handle standing out like that. I worked so hard all the time to fit in and sound like everyone else, and then the proud Greek parents would show up and, in an instant, bring me back to where I was the first day I set foot in this country.

A decade and a half later, on my first day at the executive boardroom table at Maritz (a career step I will say more about in the chapter "Work"), I was trying to quash a different kind of panic attack: I was surrounded by articulate and refined communicators, all of them Canadian-born and with no accents. I felt inferior, and I was nervous every time I tried to say something. It took a long time for me to develop enough confidence to be an equal participant around that table.

Integration was an agonizing struggle for me, particularly because of my neuro-atypical tendency to view things as strictly black or white. My mind didn't easily grasp nuances, and I assessed things only as good or bad, in or out. As a young immigrant I was naturally hungry to claw my way in and to be accepted by my new tribe, but for me it was an all-or-nothing pursuit, with no gradients, no shades and no room for compromises. Every little setback, every elevator embarrassment, every articulation stumble would feel like another sudden fall to the bottom of the well.

Canada was my chosen home, and its special brand was meant to completely (re)define me. I had run away from a lot of discomfort, presumed shame and ugly sensory over-load in my birth society of Greece and I was craving acceptance in my gentle new country. And I needed it to happen instantly, because of who and how I was. I worked in such ridiculous ways to bury my original identity and to over-promote my new one. I never renewed my Greek passport. I walked around with maple leaf prints on my T-shirts, my hats, even, one summer, my shorts. I flipped my "we" and "they" pronouns the moment I left Greece, anglicized my first name to Andy (and later Andrew, to sound more grown-up and sophisticated), dove into study-ing Canadian politics, read our national newspaper cover to cover every single day and inhaled every ounce of pre-cious content on the CBC. And still, even with all that, my integration project always felt precarious and unfin-ished. I spent decades worrying that I looked or sounded less Canadian, less aware, less connected and especially less articulate than my new compatriots. It was an all-consuming race to an elusive finish line.

A startling incident in my mid-forties made me revert to my legal first name. I was serving on the board of a prominent Toronto charity and we were hosting a dinner for some of our most important donors. One of our guests, a gentle, well-known, wise and particularly pleasant man named Bob Foster, happened to sit across from me at one end of the long table and began to ask me questions about my origins, my career and my life in general. When I was done sharing the twisted life story, he looked at me with a very warm smile and said: "I like everything about you and your story, except for one thing." Filled with intrigue, I asked what that might be. "Your name," he replied. "I don't like your name. What is a Greek man doing in Canada, in the twenty-first century, calling himself a fake name like Andrew?"

I was speechless. Really? Why does it matter? Did I even have an option? And even if I had, back when I was a lonely teenaged immigrant, that choice had long been erased with time. I was Andrew to everyone. Google, social media, industry publications, newspaper articles—the world only had one name for me. And before I could process any of this, Bob continued: "Change it back to your real name— tonight!"

Joe and I huddled under an umbrella as we walked home that beautiful autumn night, incapable of deciding whether to obey that friendly stranger's command. The whole thing made so much sense but was also impossibly daunting. We decided to sleep on it.

We woke up the next morning and realized it was my name day—St. Andreas's (or St. Andrew's) Day. Then we got into a cab and headed to the airport, where, for the first and only time in my life, I was denied boarding a flight because the name on my photo ID (Andreas) didn't match the name on my airline booking (Andrew). On St. Andreas's Day, no less! And on the morning after that friendly, passionate command! We both instantly felt the decision had been made for us through the clearest possible sign in the universe, and the name-reclamation process was launched.

My agonizing aversion to being a foreigner came to an end only when I finally found my own voice as a social entrepreneur. For the first time in this gorgeous life journey, I had earned my very own brand and I was truly defined by it. Every one of my other bequeathed or acquired labels was still just as valid and valuable—I was still Canadian, still a Greek immigrant, still gay, still partnered, still educated, still a musician—but they suddenly felt like foundational elements, not unique and personal differentiators. My real value to this world and my genuine reason for being were much more distinct. My burgeoning role as a social entrepreneur was fuelled by a passion to change the world, and it was that passion that helped shape my real label and finally extinguished my phobia about being an outsider. Having a real purpose and pursuing a real dream now made me feel as perfectly Canadian as anyone. Nothing else mattered, because nothing else should matter—I finally "owned" my chosen home country.

I've often said that the one thing that truly bonds us as

Canadians isn't our skin colour, our place of birth, our language or our religion (the typical national qualifiers in most other places)—it's our shared national value of unconditional mutual respect. That is really our secret sauce as a nation, and misfits like me continue to be its biggest beneficiaries. Even though I struggled to feel it at first, I was embraced and appreciated by this beautiful society from the moment I set foot here.

Canada has become my personal project. My energy and time, aside from the things that earn me a living, are almost entirely devoted to making this country even more welcoming, even more inclusive and even more relevant to the world. I actively support a national organization that helps accelerate the economic integration of professional immigrants into our country. And I've focused a great deal of my passion, time and money on another national charity that specifically supports our incredible inclusiveness, diversity and pluralism. In fact, in case you missed it on the cover, I am proudly donating all the proceeds from this book to the wonderful 6 Degrees initiative as my tiny contribution to the global war on xenophobia, discrimination, prejudice and fear of the other.

HOME

I WAS BORN A NOMAD AND A HUNTER. I escaped my home, country and continent because I was different in so many ways, but the beckoning distant horizon also teased me into leaving. My grandparents were immigrants, my aunts and uncles had moved or studied around the world, and my parents lived on airplanes.

Nomads may be much more versatile and creative in their definition of home, but I think we also crave it more intensely and define it more deeply than others. We attach a lot more feeling to it, and we may even derive a lot more satisfaction from its existence. And we can have multiple homes, or at least layers of homes that anchor us in unique ways and hold special meaning for us.

My first natural layer, of course, was Greece. I grew up in an acute love-hate relationship with my birth country: I loved the physical environment, the smells, the air, the water, the light and the music. But I hated the way my compatriots thought and behaved, the intimidating me-at-the-expense-of-you culture, the unrefined laws of their jungle and the loud, almost uncontrollable intensity of it all. I was always scared, and my secret isolation, particularly as a teenager, must have made that fear even worse.

By the time I moved to Canada, the negatives had almost completely overshadowed the positives, and I was elated to leave Greece forever. I didn't think I would ever miss the place I came from—and I couldn't have been more wrong. In no time at all, I found myself constantly and painfully craving the sights and sounds and smells of that gorgeous country: the beautiful mountain I used to hike up all the time, with its crisp, dry wind; the overwhelming fragrance of the thyme bushes; the bright red soil under my feet; the brilliant blue sky above me; the salty smell of the sea and the incredible feeling of that first dip into it on the first warm day of spring; the food; the sound of young and old people playing guitars and singing together late at night on the beach; the exquisite calm of bright summer mornings—such memories all added up to the most powerful homesickness.

As a kid, I had a couple of competing homes, and neither of them was my parents' rented house. The first was our little town of Papagou, which was just a bland, fairly new suburb of Athens. It had been designed after the Second World War as a subdivision for military families but had quickly grown into a comfortable, uniform middle-class suburb with its own ecosystem of schools, markets, restaurants, movie theatres and parks. Papagou was at the eastern edge of Athens, right at the foot of one of the three mountains that frame that megacity. And our house was literally the last on the edge of town, right at the foot of the mountain. I think my first real lover and friend was that mountain. I bonded with it from the time my dad used to take us on long hikes, but I really fell in love when I started exploring it on my own. I was always alone up there, and I never felt scared. I would hike vast distances, way up to the top and across the whole spine of it; every peak, every trail, every giant boulder had special meaning for me. The little bit of free time I had, outside of school and piano, I would devote to my buddy, the big mountain. One day I found a car that had been driven along a rocky trail and dumped at the bottom of a ravine, high up on the mountain; naively fearless as I was, I opened the door, found the registration, ran home and called the police, who discovered that the car had been stolen a few weeks earlier. The grateful owners came to our house to thank me for finding it—and they even brought me a gift!

My other nest early in life was the magnificent fortress town of Monemvasia, in the south of Greece. My mom's sister had stumbled across it as a budding architect in the 1960s and, together with her future husband, ended up making it the main project of her career and life. Monemvasia was one of the best-fortified medieval towns in that part of the world, perched on the side of a giant rock, right off the eastern coast of the Peloponnese. The rock was connected to the mainland by just a tiny causeway, hence its name, which means "single entrance" or "single access" in Byzantine-era Greek. Because it was such a tough place to conquer, over time it evolved into a uniquely diverse, multi-layered collection of architectural styles from each of its occupiers through the Middle Ages. Venetian, Ottoman and Byzantine building treasures filled the town, but when my aunt discovered it, most of them were in ruins. By the middle of the twentieth century, a new town was blossoming across the causeway, on the mainland, and it was a much more convenient place for people to live, so all but maybe a dozen of the local families had abandoned the castle on the rock. The ruins of splendid old palaces, churches, mosques and schoolhouses were nothing more than worthless stones to the locals, and the only parts of the town that remained fully standing were its beautiful walls. They wrapped around an astonishing blend of history, beauty, misery, poverty, ghosts and scorpions. Oh yes, legions of scorpions thrived unchallenged in the ruins and under the piles of rocks. The place had no electricity, no sewage system, no shops and no young people.

But my aunt and uncle instantly fell in love with the magic beneath that ghost town and started to imagine the rebuilding of the medieval city. They shared their dream and slowly let their passion infect government agencies, building code regulators, real estate investors and wealthy foreign tourists, triggering a gradual but magical renaissance that, over the past half a century, has helped resurrect an entire historic town in the most authentic way. Today, the "castle" of Monemvasia is a tightly managed unique resort town, filled with impeccably rebuilt five-hundred-year-old homes, spectacular boutique hotels, exquisite little restaurants and a diverse and eccentric blend of seasonal and, increasingly, permanent inhabitants. There are no cars, no roads, no lampposts, no power cables, no other outward signs of modern civilization—and there is no space, figuratively or literally, for mass tourism. It's one of my world's most sophisticated, deep and almost mysterious spots, full of thousand-year-old stories and ghosts. And, thankfully, the scorpions are almost all gone, victims of the multitude of cats that came with the wealthy tourists and have thrived and reproduced within the castle's walls.

Charmed by my aunt's stories, my parents took us there on a summer vacation when I was six years old. Back then, with no power and many more scorpions than kids, the place felt a bit like a prison, but it wasn't long before Monemvasia's special energy drew us in. We went back the next summer, and then every summer after that. The "submarine atmosphere," as my mentor and friend Mimis once described it, of feeling almost trapped together with everyone else inside the castle's walls quickly became one of life's sweetest addictions. In fact, one summer we literally got trapped in there. While the precious causeway was being rebuilt, massive waves during a huge windstorm wiped out the temporary gravel bypass that had kept us connected with the rest of the world, and we found ourselves stranded on the island and in the castle. There was no way in or out, and the winds and waves were so ferocious that we couldn't even get food supplies delivered to us by boat. The whole thing probably lasted only a few days, but to us kids it sure felt like the most dramatic siege in the history of Monemvasia.

This was the second home that so deeply defined my childhood. It couldn't have been more different from my flat, vanilla, middle-class suburb in the big city, and I was inspired by the enormous contrast between my two worlds. Both of them shaped me in myriad ways, but it was Monemvasia that gripped my soul, as it did Joe's from the moment he first set foot there many years ago. It is our mystical second home, drawing us back summer after summer, even from the other side of the world.

After high school, the intensity of the emotions and experiences around my escape from Greece and family made it a lot easier for me to define Canada as my new home. The contrast between Athens and Brandon could hardly have been greater, but within the span of only a few years, the quiet, simple, rural province of Manitoba had become my new home and left an indelible stamp on me. My real Canadian immersion took place in the social halls, murky rivers, blinding blizzards, flat farms and big, innocent smiles of the prairie world. I couldn't easily escape to anything familiar; the country of my origins was very far away. (And back then, phone calls across the world were exorbitantly expensive.) Everything was new and different and thoroughly exciting for someone as hungry for change and validation as I was. My new world hugged me, nurtured me, liked me and, above all, respected me. That was more than enough for me to really fall in love, to dive in with all my passion and make it all mine. Manitoba will always be home, in the most meaningful of ways.

My move to Toronto in 1986 was also a bit of an escape. It had been less than a year since the coming-out drama with the family, and things were far from comfortable for me at home. My first serious boyfriend, Dave, was decidedly unwelcome whenever one of my parents was visiting us in Winnipeg (which, because I was living with my brother and also because of everything else that had happened, was almost all the time).

When my brilliant boss challenged me to find my way into an MBA program (more about this later), I purposely looked at business schools anywhere but Winnipeg. I settled on McMaster University, and Dave and I packed our bags, our cars and our cats and drove away to Toronto. It was a bold move of defiance towards my still tender and equally threatening parents; and it was also very exciting to be leaving my safe first Canadian "nest" province and heading into the intimidatingly busy core of the country. I remember the final couple of hundred miles, as we were approaching Toronto from the north on a typically muggy, hazy summer day: going from the cool, quiet two-lane country highway to more and more lanes of cars, more and more frenzy and noise, and heat and humidity and pollution. It felt entirely appropriate: big-city boy was returning to his busy roots, after having grown up so much through his five-year retreat in the humble Canadian hinterland. I was ready to do a lot more, live a lot more and devote myself to a much faster race. That gradual increase of pace as we drove down Highway 400 towards the big city was so perfectly symbolic of what lay ahead.

But Toronto didn't become home for a while. For the first several years, until long after I met Joe, my heart still belonged under the big sky of Manitoba. I felt like a tenant in Toronto. I was good at using everything the big city had to offer me, and I definitely wasn't going to leave again, but it just didn't quite feel mine. From my mid-twenties until my late thirties I lived in the same building, on Toronto's harbourfront, and loved the experience, the convenience, the views, the neighbourhood, the busyness, the big wild parties, the bachelor lifestyle. I lived big and fun. As I progressed in my career and could afford more, I kept moving up in that building, into more expensive and more impressive condos. My final move in that building was into a gorgeous and gigantic penthouse unit, way above the lake, with views all the way across to Niagara Falls.

I was proud of my sexy nest and energized by it—I spent a small fortune furnishing it and making it feel like the ultimate party pad—and then I woke up one morning and realized how weird it was for a single, busy, career-absorbed guy to be living in such an enormous space. I hardly ever cooked, I couldn't possibly cope with the hassle and stress of hosting dinner parties, and yet here I was, bragging about living in the ultimate entertainment pad. And of course my mind leapt straight to solution mode: instead of regretting my expensive decision, I simply walked a few blocks to one of Canada's top chef colleges and put up a bunch of notices on their bulletin boards, offering advanced chef students free room and board in exchange for work as a live-in chef. Before I knew it, my phone was ringing off the hook and the candidates were lining up keenly. And bachelor boy ended up acquiring his own fabulous live-in chef at the start of each school year, for free.

But no part of that incredible journey through my twenties and thirties ever really made me feel at home. Not until the most fundamental epiphany of my entire life, late one night in the company of the moon high above Africa in the spring of 2001.

Just over a year earlier, my mom had died of a sudden

heart attack while visiting me in my big harbourfront condo. She was still young and cool and fun—and I was devastated. Her death completely shifted my axis. I started wondering what really mattered in life. I was struggling to reconcile all my new questions and feelings with the way I had been living. I saw that I had fallen into the too conventional, narrow pursuits of an immigrant to North America: jobs, career, savings, material possessions, retirement plans and more of the same. Why had saving money for retirement become almost more important than freedom today? Since when had spending more to look better and live richer become an imperative, not a choice? I wondered how much convention may have defined my mom's final years and how many different choices she might have made with her time if she had known she would drop dead at sixty. Would she have taken more than a week off work to go visit her son in Toronto that year? Would she have conformed even less and done even fewer of the routine and required things that seemed to fill her life? Would she have spoken differently to Nikitas or me or even to our dad? Would she have drunk and smoked less—or more? The deepened understanding of mortality that comes with the departure of a parent inspired me to reflect on how I once was, how she once was. How would I like to live and behave and feel if I knew I would die the next day? I dreamt of a whole different form of freedom, another level of strategic insubordination towards the rule makers of society. I still think that this abrupt wake-up call was the best gift my mother left me by dying so unexpectedly, so young and so close to me.

Project One was to bail on my career—and it sure felt (again!) like diving off the edge of the highest diving board. To the horror of my conformist, career-defined and conservative MBA buddies, I simply exited their world and threw myself into a year of discovery. I wanted to slow down, read, write, connect, ride my bike, get fit, get lazy, fall in lust or in love, enjoy my "home" and get to know myself. I could definitely afford a year of going backwards (by their sadly superficial and conventional definition), so I held my breath and took the plunge. No more glamour and paycheques and hundreds of employees. No more dull comfort, predictable alarm clock, work wardrobe and daily commute to an office. No more ego-boost of feeling wanted or needed. And no more empty but gloating proclamations of being oh so busy. Now I would have time to write, to think, to inhale the newspaper front to back every morning at the neighbourhood coffee shop, to cycle thousands of miles in a summer and to "waste" hundreds of hours on the beach.

I began this big, long life-pause by jumping on a plane to South Africa, to meet my very special newborn goddaughters (more on them later), with a stopover in Greece so I could spend some time with my recently widowed and rapidly mellowing dad. After a few days with him in Athens, I took a quick side trip to the island of Crete, where Joe and I had made some fun friends on a trip a few years earlier. At this point, Joe and I were just best friends and no longer lovers— we had declared the end of our romantic relationship nearly ten years earlier—so I showed up in Crete as a single, relaxed, unemployed, playful and willing dude from Canada. In no time, a fun fling ensued with the gorgeous young brother of one of my hosts, who was serving in the Greek marine forces. And, perhaps predictably, the young marine was a bit upset when it was time for me to move on to South Africa. There were lots of questions as to why I wasn't extending my stay or why I wasn't at least planning to stop in Crete again on my way back to Canada, to which I replied (repeatedly) that I couldn't plan for that, because eventually I'd have to get back "home."

When I got to Durban, the same drama played out again: a beautiful little fling with the beautiful young brother of someone I knew there, with a similar torrent of tears at the end of the visit and questions about why I couldn't stay longer. And, once again, the same uncomfortable response from me: it was simply time to go "home."

And then came the fateful moment. My flight back left Johannesburg late at night and we headed north, right through the middle of Africa. I was sitting by the window, looking at the gigantic full moon over the mysterious continent that had always fascinated me. Everyone around me seemed to be asleep, but I was awake and my mind was racing. All the fun of the previous few weeks, the lust, the discoveries, the endless appetite and then the separations and all those silly tears. Twice! And both times my response was identical: I couldn't stay longer because I had to get back "home." What was that all about? What was really drawing me back? Was it my town? My condo? My friends? My routines? My possessions? My cats? Why the heck was I cutting short all the freedom and exploration that I had so hungrily chased?

Maybe it was the moon or the setting or the sweet loneliness of that moment, but something finally helped me get it: I had grown up! I had clawed my way a little higher up on Maslow's pyramid. "Home" was finally defined by love, not by geography or a lifestyle. It was a person, not a town or a penthouse condo or a job or an island castle. Life had already presented me with my final, real and permanent home—and it was my beautiful lover, my best friend, whose soul had become so irreversibly intertwined with mine, even though he and I had spent the previous decade in strange denial.

LOVE

AS A CHILD, I always admired my parents. I thought they were the hippest, smartest and sexiest parents any kid could have. They were cooler than all my friends' parents: they spoke differently, they lived and looked younger, they travelled everywhere, they hosted funky parties, they knew so much more and, above all, they seemed so deeply connected to each other. Their emotional intimacy both fascinated and intimidated me. It seemed impenetrable, perfectly private and immensely powerful. At first I just admired it, along with everything else I admired about them. But over time, as my hormones began to flow and my insecurities began to explode, I started to envy it. Apart from the crushing sexual-orientation "deficit" I felt compared with their supposedly normal lives, I became convinced that I would never be as soul-connected to another human being as they were with each other. And that feeling of never being able to live as well and feel as fulfilled as those who had created me became one of the heaviest weights on my soul and on my self-confidence right through my adolescence.

I never tried to rationalize that gap in my own expectations, and I certainly never talked to them about what it took to build their bond; I just marvelled and studied them in silence. But as my hidden envy blossomed, so did my childish and neuro-atypical attempts to invent my own circles of emotional intimacy. I would look at every new friendship as an opportunity for that type of magical mental connection with someone—and the excitement would drive me to dive into every new connection with unfiltered and often extreme intensity; I would overtrust and overinvest without even checking for a hint of reciprocation. I would do the same with older relatives, aunts, uncles, even faraway family friends, whom I drew into becoming my pen pals. And I would write and phone and meet and talk endlessly, always hoping to find a way to feel as tightly connected to another soul as my parents obviously felt with each other. My teenage years were defined by this frenzied search for love and connections everywhere. At a time when the spectrum of autism was so much less understood, nobody attached any label to all these exceptional behaviours. I was simply considered a bizarrely hypersocial kid.

My early move away from home opened up a range of possibilities but didn't change my style or momentum. I was still anxiously looking for love, and still feeling deficient and deprived in that respect, but at least now I was a young adult, living unsupervised and feeling a lot more "normal"—because everyone around me also appeared to be hunting for the same thing. I enjoyed my enormous capacity to open up and invest emotions in new people all the time. I thrived on it, in fact. I loved the constant adventure, the thrill of discoveries and new forms of love and connection. I plunged, and plunged often, into the silliest and shallowest of flings and friendships. I learned to substitute quantity for quality and to bury my craving for emotional intimacy way beneath my frenzied "fun" lifestyle. In short, I confused excitement with satisfaction. I drove myself so hard and fast and unearthed so many lust opportunities along the way that I managed to convince myself that I was riding the perfect wave. And as I got into my twenties, the nagging sense of envy I felt towards my parents started to fade. The old folks began to look a little more tired, a little less ideal for each other and a little less inspiring. And from my high spot, right on top of that amazing wave, I found I no longer needed to shift my eyes quite as far up to see them.

And then my entire world was reinvented by a chance encounter. It was a gorgeous spring day, Mother's Day, the fourteenth of May, 1989. I was twenty-five years old and had just completed my second degree and started my first real job. I had spent that morning cleaning up the big mess from a rowdy party I had thrown in my condo the night before for a couple of MBA classmates who were getting married. I was a bit hungover and sleep-deprived and probably not looking my best. But once the big cleanup was done, I threw on the cheesiest pair of red shorts and an ugly T-shirt and drove to Toronto's Greektown for lunch with a bunch of friends. We sat on a patio and feasted on sunshine, garlic and laughs for hours. And then, as I was driving back home and feeling the lure of a hangover-induced cozy nap in the gorgeous spring sun, I took an exit off the highway, parked the car and walked into Toronto's High Park. I spotted an empty picnic table in the middle of a sunny, grassy field.

High Park was my favourite cycling destination: it was far enough from home to be a bit of a challenging ride, and its steep hills offered some great speed and cardio thrills. I had always spent a lot of time cycling, particularly after moving to Toronto, with all its biking routes and paths along the lake. On that beautiful sunny Sunday, I was frustrated at not being able to ride; my old bike was wrecked, and I hadn't yet figured out where or how to buy a new one. (Not only was the thought of the astronomical $100 expense intimidating, but I didn't know how to bring a new bike home after driving to a store in my car.) So showing up at the park in a car made me envious of those there on bikes, although all such thoughts were quickly eclipsed by my powerful sleepiness.

As I walked over to the picnic table, I didn't even notice that there was a person sitting at the next one, with a bike by his side. It was the only other table, and he was the only other human being in that entire grassy field, but I don't even remember seeing him. I lay down on my picnic table and promptly fell asleep.

The whole time I slept, he stayed there. He just watched me, in my geeky clothes, my day-after-the-debauchery tired and ungroomed face and my very own little Greek-meal garlic cloud hovering above me and keeping the mosquitoes away. And then, when I finally woke up (still unaware of him sitting at the next table), he asked me if I had the time.

In my well-trained hunter's mind, that was the most eye-roll-worthy pickup line. But hunters can't miss opportunities, so I turned to him, told him the time (it was twenty minutes to seven) and for the first time noticed his beautiful face and his warm and genuine expression. I remember thinking, *How did I miss that before?* We started to chat. We talked about cycling. (I discovered that he almost never biked. How odd that he, a non-cyclist, would be there on a bike when I, an avid cyclist, was there without mine.) We talked about Greece (he had been there a few years earlier and had even learned a couple of impressive tongue twisters). We talked about parents, family, our recent degrees, Toronto, the weather, jobs. We kept talking for what seemed like hours.

It was getting dark and cool, and I began to worry about him cycling all the way home from there—or maybe I was looking for a reason to continue talking—so I offered him a ride home. He declined, because he couldn't imagine how to fit his bike into the tiny trunk of my car, but I kept insisting, of course. Eventually, with three-quarters of his bike precariously hanging out of the back of my car, we slowly and carefully drove to his parents' home. When we got there, he offered to meet me again someday and help me go buy a bike; his sister had a hatchback. I found a gas receipt in my car, wrote my phone number on it and sealed my fate.

That was the most important day of my life. The incredible human being who wrapped his soul and his endless love around me, who truly got me and all my weird edges, who ended up becoming my real and only home, who has shaped me so deeply and in such meaningful ways, was sitting there, on a lonely picnic table, under that glorious sun, just waiting for me to walk right past him, not even see him, and fall asleep in front of him. And, as he always does, he just waited. He wasn't hunting for anything, and even I, the relentless hunter, wasn't after anything that day. We both just happened to be there, coincidentally sharing the same love for that same gorgeous spring sun. That day and those two lonely picnic tables turned out to be the time and place for the most magical intersection of two people's lives.

We fell in love right away, though the journey was complicated right from the start. Hyper-hunter meets sensitive, mellow novice. Spoiled, determined, autonomous, autistic, hungry career-builder courts shy, ambivalent, protected family-nest boy. The wondrous intensity and magic of what we felt for each other were tested, day after day, by the opposing forces in our lives, lifestyles and genes. My parents never really accepted him. His beautiful parents didn't even need to accept me, because for the longest time they didn't know what was going on.

A few years into it, we separated, or thought we had. We were so in love with the love we were feeling for each other that we decided to find a safe and cautious way of protecting it from being torn up by the daily trials, volatilities and risks of an intense relationship between two young men who were so enormously different from each other. So we came to the brilliant decision that we would no longer be lovers—we would just be best friends. We told the world about it, and nobody seemed to believe us, but we convinced ourselves and went on pretending to be single for almost a decade. The hunter went back to his familiar ways, and the sensitive mellow novice tried to learn how to hunt as well.

We spent ten very strange years in complete denial. Our friends kept laughing at us and making bets on how long it would take for us to come back to our senses. It really was impossible to unwrap the most perfect blend of two human beings, but, somehow, we held on to the assumption that our hybrid existence was all we needed. We lived separately and dated others but never let a single day go by without speaking with each other; we could travel only together; our lives overlapped more and more and more—not out of habit or need but out of want. We felt everything I used to envy about my parents' perfect soul connection and it was right in front of our eyes, but for ten long years, we tried to pretend it wasn't there.

And then, finally, on that late-night flight over Africa, I had a moment of recognition. As it all came together, my brain started to rage with a wild mix of intrigue, relief, happiness and positive anxiety. There was so much I suddenly had to tell Joe, but I was trapped inside a plane at forty thousand feet, ten thousand miles and twenty-four hours away from home. I jumped up and asked the flight attendant for some writing paper; all she could find was a bunch of small airline notepads. I sat for hours in the quiet, dark cabin, my tray table illuminated by the tiny reading light, and shared my big *aha* with the love of my life on seventeen small, loose notepad sheets. I pretended that we still had a choice, that we could still choose to build separate lives and somehow in the background maintain a special friendship with each other. But it was obvious from the way I wrote that we didn't have a choice.

By a beautiful coincidence, I landed back in Toronto on the twelfth anniversary of that unintended pickup line in

High Park (an anniversary we always celebrated, even in our most "single" years), so it was the ideal moment for me to hand-deliver the letter. I asked Joe not to read it until after I had left his apartment—and then he stayed up all night and cried. Exactly 365 days later, on our thirteenth anniversary, we announced to everyone that they had all been right all along and we had only been pretending. (Not insignificantly, thirteen had always been Joe's favourite number, and now of course it's ours.)

Everything I admired, envied and craved as a kid, an adolescent and an insecure young adult I have been lucky enough to have. I am comfortably and confidently in love, and I've had the good fortune to have lived this way for almost my entire adult life. There's such a magical, mysterious core underneath the multiple layers of our connection, and that's the source of my contentment and confidence as a human being. The fact that I belong, that I have such a fundamental emotional nest, is perhaps the most energizing aspect of my existence and my biggest source of daily gratitude, particularly as an autistic man with so many unique edges. Joe and I have an expression that perfectly encapsulates the simplicity and the depth of fulfillment we draw from life: we look at each other, at random and ordinary moments, and just say the words "happy days." In this way we constantly remind ourselves that any average day with each other is happy. Being so united, so mysteriously connected and so inseparable is a pure and powerful source of happiness.

Not many years after Joe and I met, I made friends with a wonderful couple on my business trips to South Africa.

Derek and Louise were young newlyweds from Durban; she was my local reseller of internet security software, and he was a homebuilder and the hottest surfer on Durban's beaches. Our friendship blossomed quickly, and we had even talked about organizing a fun trip for them to visit me in Toronto. But then the most unimaginable tragedy struck: burglars broke into Derek's business one day, stole the little bit of cash he had just brought in to pay his casual workers, and shot both him and his father. Sadly, Derek's father died, but incredibly, my young and very strong friend was revived on the way to the hospital—although one of the bullets had gone through his spine and he was left paralyzed from the chest down.

I'll never forget how I felt when I went back to Durban after the accident to see them. I was afraid that I would be unable to do or even say anything meaningful, terrified of how I would feel when I was directly confronted with the heartbreaking aftermath of the attack. I feared that facing Derek and seeing the degradation in my friend's quality of life would absolutely wreck me, dim my energy and optimism, crush my passion for life and make me live in constant fear of losing what I had.

Instead, I walked out of that airport and instantly fell in love with the magical powers of human love. Derek was there waiting for me, in his wheelchair, smiling from ear to ear—truly loving life again because he wasn't alone. Louise was standing next to him, also with the biggest smile on her beautiful face, welcoming me to *their* new life. At the tender age of thirty, she had already completely embraced their new reality; she had infused Derek with so much of her optimism, she had wrapped him in so many layers of love and she was constantly discovering new and more exciting paths for their new lives. I was fascinated. I had never been so close to a human tragedy before, but I had also never had an opportunity to witness how miraculously the positive power of love can change lives.

Derek wouldn't have been alive if it hadn't been for their intense love, Derek wouldn't have been smiling, driving, picking me up from the airport, shopping, cooking, swimming, working (he had reopened his business just a month after his rehab), competing in wheelchair basketball leagues, travelling (they did come to Toronto, just a year after the attack) and even planning to have kids. Yes, kids! Within a few years of the accident, and after some fairly complex and creative IVF work, Derek and Louise became one of the first couples in South Africa to overcome such a severe disability and bring to life their own biological kids—our gorgeous twin goddaughters, Jamie and Donna.

In some ways the rich love lessons from my precious friendship with Derek and Louise helped me prepare much more for the inevitable hard moments of life. When each of my cool parents died young, it hurt a lot, but I found myself remarkably ready to manage. I knew how to be vulnerable as I leaned on Joe, and I knew how to let his love become my fuel for renewal. I was sad, but I could still smile, genuinely and a lot, about life. At the same time, reflecting on my parents' lives taught me so much about how unconstrained love can become the driving force for a great journey. My cool and rebellious parents never held back, because they loved the journey a lot more than they loved that mirage of life that we often refer to as "destination." They didn't care if they ever arrived. They never became famous or wealthy. They just lived and loved every day. Their fulfillment came from loving, not from planning. They may have never rationalized all that, and they certainly didn't pass it down to us in words, but without a doubt, I inherited their carpe diem genes, further accentuated by my neuro-abnormality—and I feel blessed.

LIFE

MY MOTHER WAS TAKING A NAP when I walked into the house, went to her room, tapped her on the shoulder and said, "Mom, I got suspended from school." She opened her eyes, looked at me, mumbled the words "That's okay," turned over and went back to sleep. And my heart rate quickly returned to normal.

A couple of days earlier, she had packed my bathing suit and told me to have a good swim on my eighth-grade school trip to some beautiful beach town. Swimming on school trips had been strictly banned all across Greece after a group of students had drowned in a horrific accident in the early 1970s. Our teachers would always warn us before each trip. As would the other kids' parents. But not my outrageous mom, who loved swimming and loved bending the rules of life even more. She packed that bathing suit for me and set me up to be the chief rebel in my class that day. Eighteen of my classmates followed me to a (supposedly hidden) beach not far from where the rest of the class was gathered for lunch, and of course it didn't take long for some of the teachers to find us frolicking in the water. We all got suspended for three glorious days, including this supposed keener of a bookworm. Most of the others ended up having to face the wrath of their furious parents. I, on the other hand, simply watched my mother yawn, turn over and continue her nap.

That's how she was built, and those were the type of genes she apparently passed down to me. She interpreted rules instead of following them. She prioritized life her way. She found and baked fun into every moment. She laughed a lot. And she loved pranks.

April Fools' Day was like Christmas in our home. We couldn't wait to outdo each other and also to gang up on everyone else outside of the immediate family. One year, when I was in high school, my mother drove us to an electronics store to buy the longest video cable available (I think it was twenty or thirty yards). We secretly ran it from our neighbour's TV, through her window, across her yard and ours, through our window and into our VCR, then retuned all her TV channels to the output frequency of our VCR, popped in one of my dad's porn tapes and simply waited for that lovely elderly, prudish and allegedly virgin woman to come home. We all huddled by the front windows and watched her walk up from the bus stop. As she always did when she got home, she changed into her robe, sat down on her sofa and turned on the TV. Her screams were so loud that we could hear them through the closed windows. Moments later she was on the phone with my mother, warning her about those "bloody communists" who had started broadcasting this stuff to everyone's home because their mission was to destroy our society. My mom was my hero again that day.

I grew up surrounded by unspoken lessons on how to squeeze the most juice out of life. And then, as my parents grew older and stiffer and as they watched me perfect their teachings and exceed their rule-interpretation accomplishments, they worried a lot about me and tried hard to pull me back. But it was too late. The journey from conscious or habitual blind obedience to "life optimization," as I think of it, was irreversible.

From the moment I left home, I was an optimizer. I invested my creative energy in figuring out how to fit as many of my favourite things as I could into my life. When I was in university and still had access to my dad's free airline passes, I would crisscross the world, just because I could. I would leave Brandon at noon on a Thursday, take the bus (or hitch a free ride) to Winnipeg, hop on a flight to Toronto, catch a late-evening flight to London, jump on a connecting flight to Athens and walk into my parents' home without any warning early on a Friday evening. After thirty-six hours of partying with my old school buddies, I'd travel another twenty hours to get myself back to Brandon in time for a good Sunday night's sleep, and turn up well rested at classes Monday morning. Each time I flew on one of his passes, my dad would see a mere eight-dollar service fee deducted from his paycheque. But the charges were adding up so fast that he began to complain and threatened to start asking me for the money.

The more grown-up versions of my life-squeezing behaviour may have been less physically draining, but they were just as intense and had just as much impact. From living in a penthouse condo that was worth almost ten times my annual pay and charging the monthly rent on my credit card so I could earn even more frequent flyer miles, to selling all my records to my little brother as soon as I had recorded them onto cassettes, life always seemed full of great opportunities to stretch, innovate and make more out of every moment. Why not, I thought, find a smart way to combine a full, or at least a fully productive, workday with a fabulous summer afternoon at the beach? (When the BlackBerry first appeared and I could get my work emails anywhere, I felt the world was finally being redesigned in my favour.) Why not figure out how to have a free live-in chef at home? And why ever miss a party, a vacation, a swim or a beautiful sunrise when all it took to squeeze them into my day was a creative interpretation of the rulebook?

My distant ancestors in Greece had a great saying: appetite increases once you start eating. The list of my favourite things may have been short and simple when I was a kid, but it has grown a lot more complex and comprehensive over the decades. The slow crawl up Maslow's pyramid has shifted the balance away from the superficial and towards the meaningful and lasting, but the intensity and style of my pursuits hasn't really changed much. And while the taste buds may have evolved, some of the most basic, natural and simple satisfiers continue to rule the average day: sunshine, cycling, beaches, hikes, numbers, weather, spontaneity, great food and, above all, people. I can thrive on my own, and I often do, but I draw all my energy from spontaneous and often unstructured interactions with others. I love learning, and I adore teaching and sharing. Two of my most favourite and basic daily rituals involve reading the newspaper front to back and then clipping (once upon a time with scissors, now through screenshots on my iPad) and sharing articles, often along with my own comments.

And of course, each year April Fools' Day still feels like Christmas.

WORK

IN GREEK, THE words *slavery* (δουλεία) and *work* (δουλειά) sound almost exactly the same and they're even spelled the same, with just a difference in the accent. While I have no expert opinion on whether the similarity in nomenclature may have somehow influenced the work ethic and productivity of average modern-day Greeks, I do remember growing up with a distinct aversion to working or investing any effort beyond the minimum I could get away with. My summer jobs during high school were defined by an almost comical mix of resentment and creative cheating. I just couldn't fathom why I should waste sunny summer days slaving away as the local plumber's assistant one year and as a production assistant at my uncle's recording studio the next. And more than anything, I couldn't cope with the structure, the routine and the predictability of it all. Why did I have to work until five each day? What good could possibly come from all those arbitrary rules? Why were they paying me for the amount of time and freedom I gave up to be at work each day instead of paying me for what I produced? I felt trapped in a box that made no sense to me.

Things weren't that much different when I got my first real job after university. My degree was in computer science and mathematics, so I went looking for programming jobs.

A good friend of mine told me about a staffing agency that was placing young programmers on contract at the shiny new data centre that Air Canada was about to open in Winnipeg, so I applied and easily got the job. Here I was, twenty-one years old, with a sexy and easy new job as the youngest computer programmer in that Air Canada building, making remarkably good money—but still feeling stuck inside a suffocating box. I got paid for being there, not for achieving.

I dreaded the routine, the slowness, the rigidness. Everyone went for coffee break together; everyone took lunch at the same time; then another coffee break; then that pathetic "goodnight" they would all say to each other as they walked out of work, even though to me that moment always felt like the beginning of my real day, not the end. Set paydays, assigned parking spots, meaningless department meetings, retirement parties—it all felt like prison. And of course there was no internet back then and no such thing as surfing at work, so I invented another method of keeping my brain awake: I had access to all of Air Canada's operations reporting systems on my computer, so I would entertain myself (and feed my insatiable hunger for numbers) by analyzing flight statistics, daily passenger loads, on-time records and—naturally—all their hourly weather reports from each airport.

I don't remember what faint hope I was hanging on to, or whether the wildness of my post–5 p.m. life dulled the pain and recharged me for the next day, but somehow I was able to keep going like this for a year and a half—and I might have lasted (and rotted) even longer had it not been for my enlightened manager, who sat me down one day and talked to me about going back to school to broaden my career options. He pointed out to me what I was trying not to notice at work each day: that I was too creative, too people-driven, too unstructured and too broad a thinker to be spending the rest of my career doing this type of "square" work. He encouraged me to get into an MBA school right away, even though I might have been a bit too young and inexperienced for some. I couldn't stop smiling. I thanked him, and thanked him again the next day, and I loved the way I felt: that square box was suddenly gone.

I zeroed in on the only co-op MBA program in North America at the time, at McMaster University. I had gotten used to making a bit of money, so the idea of working some interesting jobs in between my academic terms was irresistible. I was told that getting accepted into that co-op program would be tough because I had so little work experience, but I managed to get in. Right after my twenty-third birthday, I packed it all up, celebrated that final 5 p.m. goodnight line from that big square box and moved to Southern Ontario to start chasing the bigger dream.

All three of my MBA work terms were about as horrid as my programming job at Air Canada had been. Apparently those kinds of prison boxes didn't exist only in Winnipeg; they were just as common and just as miserable in Toronto. If anything, things were even duller for me, because I was now only a co-op student, and my employment by those large, amorphous organizations was more of a charitable act; nobody really cared if I contributed anything or if I felt useful in any way. Thankfully, they were all short gigs—less than four months each—so at least I could easily count down the weeks and the days. But the other hidden benefit was that I now had a bit of experience, some interesting new connections in the world, and a restless and vastly underused mind, so I was able to gradually invent, design and eventually pitch the perfect custom job that I would plunge into as soon as I finished my MBA.

Here is how the pieces came together: Through my ultra-dull job in Winnipeg, I had gotten to know the guy who ran the staffing agency that had employed me and, through him, I had learned a little bit about how that industry worked and how they made money. Conveniently, the agency was based in Toronto, so I was able to maintain a bit of a friendship with him during my MBA years. He was a very successful young man, not that many years older than me, and the contrast between our lives was a constant source of fascination for both of us, and an effective friendship glue. He had never gone to university, and instead had started his career in his late teens, had married and had kids young and seemed to always know exactly what he wanted in life. By contrast, I had really only worked for a year before my mid-twenties, I had no savings, I had given up a well-paying job to go back to school, and I had no appetite to follow any kind of struc-tured path in life. But beneath all that, I felt as career-hungry and as creative as he was.

So we started spending more and more time together towards the end of my MBA, and then one day I pitched to him what might have been the oddest concept he had ever heard: I asked him to hire me as his export manager. I told him that the Persian Gulf was one of the most expat-labour-dependent parts of the world, particularly in terms of technology jobs and especially with Canadians. I showed him that no other Canadian staffing firm had focused there yet. And I convinced him that if he was to start advertising positions in the tax-free countries of the Gulf, he would not only generate tremendous interest among systems professionals in Canada but dramatically expand his agency's database of candidates for Canadian clients as well. I also showed him how my salary, my travel and all our other export development expenses would be covered by a fantastic combination of federal and provincial government programs designed to encourage Canadian companies to develop export markets. The facts were all solid, and the idea was as irresistible as it was totally off-the-wall, so we shook hands and decided to go for it.

I had created a real job for myself.

The ride was outrageous and full of interesting lessons and surprises. I travelled to the Gulf and we immediately found clients; we advertised their job vacancies in Canadian newspapers; our database was flooded with new candidates (at one point a single Middle Eastern job ad in *The Globe and Mail* brought us more than seven thousand resumés); we learned how to manage extreme forms of cultural diversity and how to explain to Canadian women that they needn't even apply for such jobs in Saudi Arabia; and, above all, I learned how I was made to work creatively and differently.

I always stood out, no matter where I was: I was the different guy with that very different job when I was in our Toronto office; I was absolutely out of the ordinary, *their* ordinary, every time I sat in a meeting with clients or prospects in Kuwait or Dubai or Jeddah. The only regular thing about my work was jet lag! And, finally and very happily, I was earning an income because I was building something, not because I was simply showing up at work. I couldn't get enough of it! While most of my MBA buddies were working at investment banks up the street, I was busy interviewing IT directors twice my age and warning them about such things as beheadings, like the one I had witnessed on my last trip to Riyadh.

I also quickly fell in love with exporting. It wasn't just the travel and the little bit of glamour; it was also the unconventionality of the work and the unusual survival and success skills that were required. I loved dredging up the six words in Arabic that my mom had taught me as a kid and using them to charm my clients. I thrived at doing deals over meals instead of boardroom tables. I discovered the important and inverse correlation between physical distance and emotional proximity: the farther you are from your clients and partners, the more you need to trust and respect each other in order to be successful. The unique emotional content of my job was sweet and gratifying—so when the Gulf War broke out in 1991 and our staffing work suddenly fell apart, I found myself at another company managing their exports overseas. Different company, entirely different products (we were selling data communications equipment) and much more established internationally, but the work was just as original and inspiring for me. I was making friends all over the world, defining my own recipes for success in different cultures, inventing ways to harness the fantastic creativity and energy of our Canadian trade missions overseas and always loving the thrill of being able to stand out, no matter where and how.

Then came a third export job, at a voice recognition software firm that was ahead of its time and soon went bankrupt, and a fourth one at one of the world's first internet firewall companies. That fourth one was the wildest ride of all; we were trailblazing and working harder and faster than I had ever imagined, and I was completely absorbed by our success and by how fast I seemed to be growing, along with the company. I was still the guy with the very different job, and I still drew so much oxygen from being able to operate autonomously five thousand miles from home, but I was also enjoying a lot of the lessons that came with being part of a rapidly expanding business at the dawn of the internet era. Eventually, I opened our three little sales-and-support outposts across Europe, and I moved or hired our staff over there. I started to build a bit of a public relations function into our overseas work. And I also discovered the interesting feeling of being the guy in the company with the most significant sales numbers, because so much of our revenue was now flowing in from my European distributors, and so many eyes were trained on me at the end of each month. And I was still just in my early thirties, still a weird kid who preferred to talk about the weather and funny numbers on licence plates.

At the beginning of 1997, I got a call from a headhunter: Maritz, the successful Canadian subsidiary of a large global marketing services agency, was looking to hire an executive to lead a new but fairly significant global division. A few months earlier, they had won a contract to manage all the incentive programs for IBM's twenty-five thousand resellers and distributors across the world, a job that required setting up support centres across North America, Europe and Asia to manage hundreds of millions of dollars of IBM's marketing promotion funds and an enormous volume of exchanges and communications between giant IBM and all those resellers. The firm was searching for someone with expertise in channel marketing in the IT industry and plenty of overseas experience. I suppose that was still a bit of an unusual combo at the time, so my resumé popped up as a perfect match, and I found myself being interviewed for an executive gig that was so much bigger and different than anything I had done before.

I got the job and soon found myself swimming through the most significant, and at times the most intimidating, transition of my career. The lonely cowboy of the wild, fast but unsophisticated world of technology sales was now sitting at the executive boardroom of a global marketing agency. Only thirty-three years old and just a decade and a half off the boat, I had an army of older, experienced, smart people in locations all over the world reporting to me. This meant having to learn faster than ever before in my life, and at times, barely able to keep up, I felt a bit like Chauncey Gardiner in *Being There*. I thought I looked too young, acted too inexperienced and spoke in too unsophisticated a manner to deserve that kind of job, but in the end, my intense fear of being "found out" served as the best propulsion fuel: I thrived in that job, made a career home for myself and have since often referred to my years at Maritz as my second and much more important MBA.

Apart from all the great work and growth, that chapter of my career also contained an unmatched level of glamour and fun. Maritz ran some of the world's most coveted corporate incentive programs, and we, as leaders in that organization, had opportunities to not only sample the goods but also, as part of our job, play host to some of our top-achieving salespeople on incentive trips. The experiences were truly amazing, and at some point Joe and I lost count of the number of helicopter rides we had taken in various corners of the planet. We saw extraordinary places; travelled in submarines, private limos, seaplanes and luxury yachts; enjoyed sensational meals; opened top-end bottles of wine; and stayed in some of the world's best hotels. It felt like in the blink of an eye I had travelled from the deepest jungle of the IT world to the sophisticated peak of the marketing services industry.

Then came my young mom's sudden death and that significant shifting of my axis. I woke up one day questioning the entire conformist rat race, and decided to exit my career.

And off I went. I felt inspired, strong, confident and smart enough to blow up all my routines in the pursuit of living a fuller life. I learned how to count breaths, smell flowers, really connect with my people and—more importantly than anything else—rank the most valuable elements of my life. That ranking exercise happened so fast that within six weeks of leaving my career I had already written that seventeen-notepad-page letter on that long, quiet night flight over Africa, and I knew exactly who was meant to be holding my hand through the journey of the rest of my life.

I took a whole year off. For twelve months I invested energy in everything except my career. I didn't look for work; I didn't even have an answer for those who asked what I would do next. The whole conventional world around me doubted me and tried to talk sense into me. My dad couldn't comprehend it and eventually gave up asking questions. But Joe got it, loved it, quietly admired it and kept feeding my passion and courage to be different. He watched me grow through that year and knew that good things would come of it.

Even on the conventional side of life, great things came from it. My next real job, after a couple of post-sabbatical consulting gigs, was my first experience in the CEO seat. Would I have gotten there if I hadn't stepped right out of the scene and taken that huge, year-long breath? I'll never know the answer, but I'll never forget how tuned in and grown-up I felt when I was being interviewed for the job. The executive boardroom table underdog of just half a dozen years earlier had been transformed into a confident communicator who knew how to draw in smart people. My fear of being found out as the littlest and weirdest guy at the table had been replaced by layers of pride and a solid sense of being fully in control: I was ready to sit at the head of the table, harness the more conventional brilliance of those who sat with me and wrap it around my unique skills.

For the next few years, I ran Gorrie Marketing, one of the oldest retail marketing agencies in Canada. It really was an old shop, 125 years old, in fact, full of piled-up legacy headaches and hungry for new energy—and I was as odd a leader for it as the place was old. Going in, I had no idea how complicated and interesting it would be to work as a hired-gun CEO in such a well-entrenched family business, nor did I realize how much creative diplomacy it would take to manoeuvre through it all each day. I had to deploy and nurture three separate personas all the time; I needed to belong to the family, to some extent, in order to understand their anxieties and habitual priorities; I needed to "get" all the legacy attitudes and deep-rooted habits of the people who had been with that firm for a very long time, so that I could communicate with them convincingly in their own language; and I needed to be seen as the passionate builder and driver of new ways of being and behaving at the firm. At any moment, in any conversation, whether with our people or with clients, I needed to be able to switch instantly and seamlessly between these three modes. It was a lot of work, particularly in the early months, and I found it utterly fascinating.

One of my most meaningful sources of support and growth during the Gorrie years was my new network of friends at the Young Presidents' Organization. I had always heard amazing things about YPO and had always craved joining it. The moment I took the reins at Gorrie and finally qualified, based on my role and the size of the business I ran, I jumped in. It turned out to be one of the most transformative decisions I ever made, not just for my career but for my life in general and for our life at home as a family unit. I quickly learned that the main purpose of YPO wasn't to be a social club or a career-support group: it was to simply create opportunities for us to learn from each other and grow faster as leaders in society. Our focus is a lot broader than just careers. We connect and share and learn in order to make ourselves better in every way: better role models, better builders of our homes and families; and, of course, more inspiring leaders for our people at work.

The other remarkable thing about YPO is its balance between energy inputs and outputs. It's a volunteer organization and it comes with no preconceived requirements of the amount of time and energy each member should be investing, but the rate of emotional return for each of us is directly proportional to what we put in. The more we offer into it, the more growth we get out of it.

Joining YPO as the first openly gay Canadian member was fascinating. Such a well-established and prominent group of overwhelmingly male CEOs could so easily be defined by its testosterone quotient and would most likely feel a lot like a boys' club, so I was quite keen to figure this out before I signed up. I asked to go to lunch with Ron Close, who was the chair of the Toronto chapter at the time. In the long and jagged journey of my life as a gay businessman, that lunch chat with Ron will always stand out as one of the most validating and energizing moments. He looked me straight in the eye and, with a big, genuine smile, very firmly said, "We need you." We talked about the need for much more diversity right across that powerful club, and Ron passionately challenged me to join and become a local, national and global champion for openness in all its forms.

And so I plunged right in, with Joe right by my side all the time, at every event, every trip, every disruptive appearance and conversation. For a childless newbie member couple like us, there were endless opportunities to get involved—and for the country's first out couple, the amount of attention we attracted quickly became our unique fuel. People started to invite us to lead events, to speak about our experiences, meet and inspire their kids, take on more visible roles in the organization and generally get more involved. We both had the time and the appetite. And the snowball kept growing. Within a (record short) couple of years, I had become the chair of the Toronto chapter. A year later I was the membership chair for Canada. I helped spawn some common-interest global networks and ran global conferences, and suddenly a big chunk of our social life was wholly absorbed by YPO. It was an inspiring new chapter and, perhaps not surprisingly, it redefined the direction of the rest of my career.

GREEN

ON THE LAST DAY OF MAY 2007, I got on my bike and cycled all the way up to the northern fringes of Toronto to have lunch at the home of a man I barely knew. His name was Dean Topolinski, and he was perhaps the best-known misfit in YPO's Toronto chapter. He worked out of his home, together with his brother, who lived next door to him; in fact, the two were so close that their houses shared one backyard and were essentially a compound for their two families. He did some very strange work with distressed assets: he bought up badly broken businesses for pennies on the dollar, and his only project was to fix them up, and in some cases break them up, then dress them up and sell them for better money. He appeared to be a gentle, warm soul, but people had already spoken to me about his sharp "teeth" and his exceptionally tough negotiating style. He was definitely a polarizing member of our chapter; many loved him and some even went into business deals with him, while others didn't want to have anything to do with him.

I was excited to be going to Dean's, not only because of his spicy reputation but also because he had agreed to chair the most important and fun event of the following year for our YPO chapter. I was in charge of all our events for that year, so it was my job to make sure people like Dean knew what they were supposed to be doing and followed through on their commitments. So in essence I was heading into a meeting with this controversial and somewhat legendary YPOer I hardly knew to simply "manage" him and to tell him what to do for us. That he had offered to meet over a great lunch served by his live-in chef added a little extra horse-power to my northbound pedalling.

The beginning of our lunch chat was full of energy, fun and smiles. We had met only once before, with a group of other YPOers, so this was our first opportunity to get to know each other one-on-one. The conversation was mostly personal—about our spouses, his kids and our hobbies. We eventually got to talking about the planned event and sorted it out fairly quickly. Then we launched into a bit of business talk. My interest in his work was obvious, and he seemed rather curious about how I had gotten to where I was.

A few months earlier, after a lot of coaching and hand-holding by some of my closest friends in YPO (my "forum mates," as we call them), I had mounted a complicated cam-paign to buy Gorrie Marketing. I had grown more and more restless with my job as a hired gun in such a family-intense organization, and I had solicited my mates' thoughts on how to make things better—or how to exit. Their consen-sus was that not only was I at the right age and stage in my life, I was also in the right environment and the right industry, and I had the right energetic executive team to be able to buy the business from the family. I was inspired and soon got to work on it. I met with investment bankers, put together an attractive package, engaged my superb team in total confidence and pulled the trigger. Unfortunately, and perhaps not surprisingly, the family was not tempted by our offer.

I was left pondering my future and also helping my superbly loyal former teammates figure out new jobs for themselves. Obviously, we all felt disappointed that we hadn't ended up owning that business, and I remember also feeling a great dose of guilt for having pushed things as far as I did and causing so much upheaval in the careers of my most senior people. At the same time, the debacle gave me a newfound freedom and the mental space to incubate new ideas. And that's how I found myself sitting in my backyard one beautiful spring morning, dreaming up something so different and, as it turned out, so transformative for my life and career.

The spring of 2007 was, without a doubt, the peak of the "green frenzy" in North America. Al Gore's movie *An Inconvenient Truth* had succeeded in bringing conversations about climate change into the mainstream, and suddenly, all my fellow marketers across the continent were scrambling to figure out how to paint their products, their companies, their jobs and their talks with as much green colour as they could find. The trend was explosive, and the tricks to riding that big green wave were simple and obvious—a bit too obvious and a bit too vanilla, I thought. It bothered me that everyone was doing the same thing, reacting the same way and simply relying on the intensity of their apparent greenness and the volume of their screaming in order to steal a tiny bit more of the spotlight from the next guy. It was too simplistic, ephemeral and myopic. At this rate, I thought, the whole green thing would become nothing more than another forgettable spike, another fad. Consumers would quickly tire of it and move on to something else that inspired them or at least caught their eye.

In the meantime, however, from looking at some market research, I was noticing something else that intrigued my climate-obsessed mind: The biggest influencer of consumer attitudes and behaviours was not a change in the eco-packaging of their favourite detergent or soft drink but the freaky weather outside. Billions of consumers around the world were beginning to respond to symptoms of climate change much more than to cheesy TV ads about cleaner-burning gasoline for their giant SUVs. And, of course, my special advantage was that I understood much better than almost all my fellow marketers that the symptoms of climate change we were seeing in 2007 were nothing compared with what we would be seeing a decade later. I was enough of a weather geek to figure out the trend lines and to know that, in terms of our weather-weirding, we were still at the very start of an incredibly steep, hockey-stick-shaped curve.

So if the worst (or most bizarre) was yet to come, and if it was true that those signals from the heavens had the biggest influence on the thinking and the shopping behaviour of the masses, then it was safe to conclude that we were at the very beginning of a marketing megatrend. Almost all the big marketers in the world were seeing this green thing as a fad, like square-toed shoes or miniskirts, to be exploited as fast as possible. But it wasn't. I understood that we were only at the start of something more fundamental, permanent and huge. And I began to realize that, perhaps for the first time in my career, I enjoyed a special advantage and I had a niche I could exploit.

I started to think about how I could build a big, new idea, a new kind of business designed to grow along with this emerging megatrend, instead of just trying to ride a short-term wave. I felt grateful that my lifelong obsession with weather and climate may have proved relevant.

Through my years at Maritz and a consulting stint at Canada's main frequent flyer rewards program, I had gotten to know the incentives and loyalty marketplace quite well. I understood why consumers were so responsive to smart incentives and particularly how popular and effective reward points were in a society like ours. So, in my scramble to invent the next big, long-term "green" thing, I came up with the idea of building a "green points" program.

I did a quick scan and confirmed that nobody in any of the leading markets in the world had yet created any kind of an eco-rewards program, one that would reward consumers only when they made environmentally responsible purchasing choices. The idea was so simple, and the void so obvious, that I began to worry: Was I missing something? Could there be a reason nobody had come up with this before? Could it be that, somehow, the economics didn't work or the effect on consumer behaviour would be negligible? And even after I dug deep and convinced myself that there were no simple or obvious show-stoppers and that I simply happened to be the first weird, climate-aware business guy to think of such an idea, I still worried about the length of my runway: With the market so obsessed with green, what if someone, somewhere else, was thinking of the same idea at the same time? What if they had more money and connections or much more of an existing platform to turn their idea into a real thing? What if I had just come so close to being an inventor of something, for the first time in my life, but the stars weren't completely aligned for me?

So the tempo and the excitement went up rapidly. I sketched out a program, to try to figure out the real money and the opportunity behind it, the mechanics of it and, of course, the market. Canada seemed like both the best and the worst place to try to do this. Best because no country in the world appeared to be more points-happy than mine; Canadians were known to drive across town for a double-points special at the grocery store, and the consumer loyalty industry in our country was worth many billions of dollars per year. Worst because all this success had created amazing entrenchment and consolidation among the leading players in this industry in Canada, so the prospect of being a tiny niche entrant in a space of powerful, entrenched and wealthy giants was intimidating in the extreme. Plus, truth be told, although I may have always played and behaved and thought like an entrepreneur, I had never imagined myself as one—in fact, I was terrified of the idea. Me, on my own, building on such a big fantasy of an idea, starting a company, chasing billion-dollar customers and fighting off billion-dollar competitors? I couldn't imagine it.

But I certainly *could* imagine someone else doing something with my idea. The one thing I had confirmed was that my idea was unique, hot and current, so someone, somewhere, needed to do something with it. I spoke with Joe about approaching the president of my old, beloved Maritz (a friend); or the president of Aeroplan, the frequent flyer program where I had once consulted (an acquaintance); or the president of Air Miles, the biggest points program in my country (also an acquaintance). Maybe there was a way to sell them my idea and have them nurture it and build it on top of their powerful platforms. I also spoke with some of my venture capital friends, the same ones who had helped me raise the money to try to buy Gorrie. There was lots of fascination with the concept of a national eco-points program, and lots of very smart questions, but no one had any specific ideas about what to do with it next.

So here I was, in the middle of lunch at Dean's house, having interrogated him for quite a while about his businesses, and now it was my turn to talk about mine. He knew that I had tried to buy my old company and failed, so his question had a bit more of a forward-leaning tone: "What are you working on?" I smiled and suddenly realized that this strange and friendly shark across from me might make a great sounding board. He knew absolutely nothing about my industry, so his advice could be perfectly unbiased and balanced. I asked him if he had the time to suffer through a bit of a download of a detailed idea. He responded enthusiastically, so I invoked our standard YPO code of confidentiality and dove right in.

Five hours later we were still sitting at his dining room table. It had been quite an afternoon. We had gone deeper and deeper into my idea; he had tried, creatively but unsuccessfully, to punch holes into it from all possible angles; I had thoroughly enjoyed the grilling; our tones and temperatures had gone way up at times. And in the end, here we were, doing something I would never have imagined as I was cycling up to his house earlier that day: we were shaking hands and agreeing to chase the most bizarre business dream together. In some mysterious way, I had found my weird match: another misfit, another passionate nonconformist, another hyperenergized and energizing dreamer. He knew next to nothing about my world, my work, my successes and failures before, and I knew next to nothing about his—but, in a totally heretical manner that would make a conventional business leader's skin crawl, we were shaking hands on a twisted, unorthodox and fun new partnership.

We would do this on our own: we wouldn't partner with the big boys, we wouldn't look to sell the idea—we would simply go and build a brand-new points program for Canada, and we'd do it in the most disruptive way possible. In a space filled with money and very wealthy competitors, we would pick the loudest and most visible David-versus-Goliath fights, on purpose, in order to quickly draw attention to our very cool idea. Dean's view was that if the concept could inspire a cynical and most un-environmental business guy and consumer like him, then it had some serious legs.

So, on May 31, 2007, Green Rewards was born. It had been conceived in my sunny backyard a couple of weeks earlier, and it was born through our amazing five-hour debate at Dean's dining room table. He would fund it; I would run it. We would follow our own custom-designed method of only gradually turning on the risk tap, one tiny step at a time; the more we figured out and the more we validated, the more we would invest in it. And, for an extra dose of sizzle and inspiration for both of us, we proudly built our fifty-fifty partnership on just a handshake, without a single piece of paper.

I still wake up, more than a decade later, with the realization that I was even crazier than my crazy mother—and I love feeling that way about it. What an unbelievable ride we had just launched ourselves on. Within a couple of weeks, we were already down in New York City, figuring out our technology providers for this monster we were about to build. Within a couple of months, we had already hired half a dozen expensive, seasoned, sharp and well-known leaders from the industry. And by the end of the summer, there were articles about us in the national newspapers, describing us as "the ones to watch."

The tiny snowball was quickly growing into a full-blown avalanche, just because we were both going about it in such an unconventional way, tickling and teasing the media with our dreamy ambitions, hiring prominent PR and branding agencies and charming some of the biggest Canadian loyalty gurus out of their boring and uninspiring jobs. We were the shiny new thing, and we were very good at attracting more and more influential eyeballs.

By the end of that year, we had already built the team up to about fifteen dream employees, and we were in serious talks with one of Canada's largest banks about partnering to launch our country's first real environmental credit card. Things were looking great. At the first-ever Green Rewards client Christmas party, just six months into the life of our crazy venture, we spotted business journalists snooping through the pile of name tags at the welcome table, looking for clues to who would be our launch partner brands the following year! A few days after that, at my eccentric new business partner's family Christmas party, I discovered that he had gone out that day and bought a gorgeous baby grand piano just because I was going to be there. I couldn't believe how spontaneous and different a character he was—and, of course, I couldn't believe how much my fingers hurt the next morning, after a marathon of playing, singing and celebrating the end of such an unbelievable year. We were on a high, and beyond all the noise and the progress we were making with the business, we loved how our quirky partnership had spawned such an extraordinary friendship between us. At first it was just about the thrill of putting so much trust into a business relationship with a stranger, but over time, the bigger thrill was about discovering ever more layers of compatibility, vulnerability and powerful connections between us.

Things got even wilder in the early months of 2008. Right around the start of the year, a couple of my young employees walked into my office to sound a mild alarm about a new, upstart green consumer marketing business that was also based in Toronto. While they weren't a loyalty points provider, their focus was just like ours—creating a permanent shift and a positive change by harnessing the momentum of consumerism—and they seemed to be getting a remarkable amount of attention from the media, thanks to their charismatic and (apparently) fearless young founder, who seemed to be charming every radio station and newspaper in the country. The little firm was called ClickGreener, and their concept was almost as simple as ours: if you did your online shopping by going through their portal, they would donate half the affiliate fees they earned from all the major retailers to an environmental charity of your choice. A perfect win-win proposition for the average online consumer: shop wherever you want to shop and buy whatever you planned to buy, but make a difference by triggering a meaningful donation each time you shopped online through ClickGreener, without having to spend an extra penny. Even though they really weren't a competitor for us, we were concerned that the attention they were getting in the media could compromise our shiny position as the star green kid of Canada's corporate world.

My colleagues arranged for me to have lunch with Click-Greener's founder, Owen Ward. While for me this was just another lunch date, I learned later that for Owen, the buildup and the anticipation were almost unbearable. I didn't know it at the time, but Owen's little start-up was truly tiny; he was a very young man, running it out of his apartment and essentially doing everything on his own, except for a few hours of help he received each week from his two minority partners. He was an energetic, genuine, warm, inexperienced and appropriately scared guy who was suddenly being asked out to lunch by the much older CEO of one of the (supposedly) most prominent green businesses in the country. He consulted with his lawyer, and even spent time planning what to wear for such an important meeting. He felt threatened even before he showed up and was ready for some sort of intense and strategic assault. Instead, he found me mesmerized by his brilliance and his passion. I just couldn't get enough of him, and I remember exactly where I was—no more than twenty yards from the door of the restaurant on my way back to the office—when I dialed Dean and told him that we absolutely needed to buy this guy's business. I didn't care much about the business, and I knew we'd have no use whatsoever for the ClickGreener model— but I couldn't wait to join forces with the amazing Owen.

It all worked out very well. It took only a couple of dinner dates between Owen and me, and then a rather memorable trip for him up to Dean's suburban home office, before we had a deal. Now Green Rewards was made up of the two crazy founders, the fifteen or so fabulous builders and a young social entrepreneur, who lived to simply change, disrupt, question, dream, stretch, inspire and care. Owen really cared: he cared about us, he cared about the real impact of the business, he cared about our clients and he cared about the world. He wore his heart on his sleeve every step of the way, and he earned the love of my entire team. We had the perfect dreamer among us, and it certainly made a difference through the rest of our unforgettable green enterprise.

Around the same time, we moved into our shiny new downtown Toronto office. In keeping with our wild trajectory since the day we launched, we picked a space that told a big, loud story about us. We took the former headquarters of a foreign bank in one of the most prestigious towers, and we looked (and felt) as if we had won the office lottery. Stunning boardrooms and offices, terrific address, lots of room for more growth and plenty of shock value and even a bit of intimidation for those who may have perhaps not taken us seriously. To add an extra dose of eccentricity into the mix, Dean gave pride of place in our main boardroom to that brand-new baby grand piano he had procured for my drunken Christmas concert a couple of months earlier. Owen played too, and Dean thought we could both release some stress from time to time, while also entertaining our bewildered employees! I still relish the thought that we may have been the only firm ever, in the heart of the financial district of Toronto, to have a grand piano right in the middle of our office. Our landlords and fellow tenants must have thought we were completely out of our minds.

The buildup continued. My colleagues were signing up dozens of eager companies that would provide fun and authentically green products and services as rewards for our expected millions of points collectors. Another team was creating partnerships with retailers who would begin offering our points to Canadians as soon as we locked in a credit card issuer (a big bank) and launched the program. And a third team was continuing to build our technology, our branding and our powerful launch plans. We had three prominent (and expensive!) marketing agencies working with us, to help dress us up and get us ready for the big national launch. The monthly bills were growing larger and larger on every front, but so was our conviction that we were positively unstoppable on our way to something great. The big loyalty giants had definitely taken notice, and the chatter in the industry media was growing ever louder. A year on, we had become really good at broadcasting updates and provoking all kinds of reactions.

Somewhere around the one-year mark, I got a call from the wife of a good YPO friend. She was in charge of corporate marketing at BMO, or the Bank of Montreal, one of our country's largest banks—and a direct competitor to the Toronto-Dominion Bank, with whom we had been dancing for the previous many months around the idea of creating an eco credit card that would offer consumers our loyalty points as rewards. BMO had historically been closely tied with the country's largest loyalty program, Air Miles, so the call from my friend's wife was both surprising and exciting. They obviously knew the loyalty game, and we knew that they were in contract renewal negotiations with Air Miles, so we assumed they were exploring ways of de-leveraging themselves a little from their dependence on a single loyalty program. We didn't hesitate for a moment, especially because we had been growing impatient with our friends at TD, and we pushed forward quickly with BMO and harder with TD.

In the span of a couple of months, the landscape had changed entirely. Our conversations with BMO escalated exceptionally fast: once they figured out how tiny and weird and potentially unstable we were, they told us they would consider getting into bed with us only if they could also have at least some ownership stake in the business. We loved it, agreed to explore it, and suddenly there were many more people at the negotiating table. Then, as we worked through the numbers, their appetite increased further, and they started to discuss taking a majority interest in Green Rewards instead of a small slice, and we continued to love it. Then their investment bankers concluded that it would make even more sense for them to simply buy the whole thing—and that's when we paused and contemplated things, because none of us had imagined becoming employees of a large, mainstream, conventional bank. But the idea of gaining that much heft and prominence in the market (not to mention the temptation of such an early exit) made our hearts flutter, so we continued to pursue it. And, once again in record time, the bank drew up a tantalizing term sheet to buy our baby that was barely a year old and had not even launched a product or earned any revenues. Dean and I were pinching ourselves; how could this be happening so quickly? Obviously, it made sense that BMO's contract renewal negotiations with the largest loyalty giant in our country were the driving force behind the rapid progress in our deal, but it was all still hard for us to believe. Armed with the confidence and excitement of a term sheet in our hands, we allowed our dialogue with TD Bank to gradually fizzle.

On June 19, 2008—a date I'll never forget—I received a request for an urgent conference call with the most senior BMO executive who was driving the relationship and the acquisition deal with us. Maurice was one of the nicest, kindest and most straightforward people I had ever done business with. He had been with the bank for all his career, and he was only a couple of rungs from the very top of that huge organization. Normally, a deal as small as ours would have been well below his level, but he had taken a passionate interest in us and in me in particular. After one of the long and complicated meetings with his investment bankers, he walked back into my office with me, closed the door, looked me right in the eye and said, "I hope you realize how proud I feel to be doing this deal with you, and I hope you know how envious I feel of everything you've been experiencing through this most recent journey." Without a doubt, this was one of the most meaningful and ego-boosting moments of my career. I already had such deep respect for that wise man, and he stole my heart when he spoke to me that way.

And now I was being asked to make time for an urgent call with Maurice, ideally within the hour, so I knew it was something serious—and I didn't feel particularly good about it. I cleared my schedule, set it up and sat there with a million scary thoughts racing through my head, waiting for the clock to finally read 4:00 p.m. so I could dial in. When I did, Maurice was already on the line waiting for me. From the tone of his greeting, I knew this wasn't going to be a happy call—and it certainly wasn't. He was calling to inform me that, most unfortunately, our deal had been vetoed from "the very top of the organization," as he put it. He was unable to share with me the reasons for that decision, other than to say, over and over again, that it had nothing to do with my business, our prospects, our team, Dean or me. He sounded almost as distraught about the news as I felt—his misery was palpable even over the phone—and he promised that some day, over a drink or two, he would have the freedom to tell me the full story, which he hoped would make me feel better. But he knew he was causing us a lot of unexpected pain by pulling the plug, and he kept apologizing for it.

I was lost. I remember putting the phone down and feeling paralyzed. My door was still closed, and outside it, all my amazing colleagues were waiting, hoping that I would come out to tell them it had been a false alarm. It was, after all, part of my job description to manage people's expectations and feelings and fears. But, for perhaps the first time in my career, I was in too much shock to do what I knew I was supposed to. I couldn't get up. I couldn't even phone Joe. What would I tell him—that our cocky trajectory and behaviour had brought us to a place where this livelihood project for us had evaporated in an instant? I simply could not face it. After ten minutes of staring at my screen and my phone and my hands and every other soothing and familiar thing in front of me, I dialed Dean.

It may have been our shortest phone call ever. All he said was, "I'll be right there," and forty-five minutes and twenty miles of rush-hour traffic later, he was walking into my office and closing the door behind him.

Obviously, I hadn't just sat there for all that time, ignoring my friends and colleagues outside that door. I gathered them all in the boardroom, and we had the big, honest conversation about the phone call with Maurice. They were as stunned as I was, but at the same time they seemed surprisingly bullish. They asked lots of smart questions about our chances of reviving the defunct dialogue with TD, about whether the whole acquisition deal with BMO might have been an unimportant diversion from our real strategy, whether going back to Plan A and really going it alone might make us all a lot happier. In a moment of crisis, they cherished their existence as a dream team and their fun work even more than the prospect of a lucrative, glamorous deal.

The first thing Dean did was to give me a big, long hug without saying anything. Then he looked me straight in the eye and reminded me of our most basic motto, which we had repeated to each other hundreds of times since the start of our wild project: Friendship first! We had agreed from the beginning that the main benefit we both saw in our partnership was the birth and growth of a deep friendship. The rest was secondary. And as soon as he put me back in the right place, I felt full of positive energy again. Could we fix this mess quickly? Probably not—and perhaps never—but I was certainly ready to try because, frankly, I had little to lose. I'd never lose him as a friend, and I'd never lose the tremendously rich memories of what we had created together, so everything else was less important. I had grown completely comfortable with the volatility and uncertainty of each week, and I was energized by every twist and surprise along the way. And that's all the call from Maurice was: another twist, another surprise in the most colourful work journey I could have ever imagined.

An hour after the chat with Dean, I was making another fateful phone call. I dialed Bryan Pearson, CEO of Loyalty-One, the company that owned and ran Air Miles. I had known Bryan through the industry, and more recently I had met him as one of our YPO newbies, so there was a new layer of comfort and trust I could invoke with him. Plus, I liked him. I didn't know him well enough to say that I trusted him, but others had told me they trusted him a lot, and I had always found him to be very warm and easy to connect with. It was way past business hours by this point, still on that fateful nineteenth of June, but I dialed his cell phone and got him right away. He and I hadn't spoken at all in the thirteen months since I had started making all that green loyalty noise across the country, but that didn't make the start of our conversation awkward in the least.

I went straight for the kill, without holding back any facts: I told him about his biggest client having circled us for months and about having gotten to the point where they had completed a term sheet to buy us; I told him about the mystery of the deal evaporating so abruptly and for a reason that could not be disclosed; and I offered to sell him the business on the exact same terms we had reached with BMO. He asked lots of questions on the spot, and we had a very open and comfortable exchange about the business, the dream, the options, the go-it-alone versus not scenarios and so on. He told me he was intrigued by the possibility and asked for a few days to discuss it with his executive team. He called me back just seventy-two hours later to tell me that his team was supportive and we should try to come to a deal. Another day, another fast turn on the rollercoaster ride . . .

In the midst of all that, however, there was one more enormous monkey wrench for me to manage: Dean's funding commitment for Green Rewards ran out. In fact, it had run out a couple of months earlier, but because the BMO deal was so close to being formalized, he and I had agreed that we wouldn't rock the boat and that he would continue cutting cheques until we were signed with the bank. So the moment the BMO deal was scrapped, his (very significant, by that point) monthly cheques also disappeared. No more payroll, fancy office, big agency payments or anything else at all—he had reached his ceiling and couldn't absorb any more risk.

I was in an unbelievable bind, having to work so creatively to keep the whole thing together while also working to accelerate our Air Miles deal as much as possible. Once again, the spectacular dream-team spirit was the highlight for me: all but one of my employees continued to smile and work as hard as they could. They knew I had never taken one penny in salary from the business, so they saw this new chapter as their turn to sacrifice a bit for the pursuit of the dream. They managed kids, spouses, mortgages and all sorts of other pressures, and almost every one of them kept showing up for work through that weirdest of summers.

Ten weeks after that call with Maurice and only two weeks before the official start of the global financial meltdown of 2008, on the second of September we completed the sale of Green Rewards to the owners of the largest loyalty program in Canada.

CRESCENDO

IT WAS A CLOSE CALL. Our deal closed on the second of September, and by the middle of that month the financial heart of the world went into convulsions. If something had delayed us by mere days, our American-owned, publicly traded buyer might have gotten spooked enough to back right out of the deal. The jitters had started some time before that. In fact, that was exactly why BMO had walked away from our original deal three months earlier. When Maurice and I finally went out in mid-September for the drink we had promised each other during that fateful phone call, he was able to tell me that back in June the bank was becoming very concerned about the darkening clouds around the world, and that was the reason for the veto, which came right from the top. Money had stopped flowing for anything that wasn't necessary, and our deal was suddenly viewed as far from essential. In many respects, we were unbelievably lucky to be able to switch horses so close to the start of the crisis and to be able to close our deal before the crash.

We spent the summer working on the assumption that Green Rewards, as a business, would be rolled into the corporate entity of the buyer. We avoided exploring the more delicate question of whether the proposed Green Rewards loyalty points program would also get rolled into the Air

Miles program or whether we might still go ahead and launch it as a separate, competitive loyalty currency. That was a question for a later time; the more urgent decisions were about how to fuse what I had built, in terms of people, technology, relationships and intellectual property, into Bryan Pearson's organization.

I was starting to feel a lot of good things about Bryan. Exhibit A, of course, was his warmth and his receptiveness when I had first called him on that dark day in June. Exhibit B was the way he supported the absorption of my business and my people. We worked hard together to find roles at Air Miles for as many of my Green Rewards colleagues as we could. In the end about half my people became redundant and got packaged out, yet only one of them was disappointed and turned litigious (and that was because, remarkably, this was his second time being terminated by Air Miles, so he was dealing with some serious career trauma). All the others whose skills or roles couldn't be transferred over to LoyaltyOne walked away happy, proud, well looked after and fully satisfied. And those who did make it across to the new company were made to feel welcome and given considerable space to build their new careers inside Bryan's much larger shop.

I remember feeling at the time that there was so much openness and trust in the way Bryan interacted with me through that summer. In fact I ended up penning an article in our national YPO magazine in which I bragged about the flavour and friendly tone of our transaction. I wrote that, with so little need to look over my shoulder during those acquisition negotiations, I probably didn't learn much about how to do a deal and had most likely set myself up to be just as naive if I ever had to sell a business again!

As soon as the deal closed, we began to work on the bigger question of whether Green Rewards, as a separate eco-points currency, should be launched at all or whether we should just take all the cool assets we had built up and weave them into the powerful Air Miles program. It wasn't an easy decision. By sticking with the original plan and launching a separate eco-loyalty rewards brand into the marketplace, we would be able to preserve its intended authenticity: it would be a true green points currency, clean and simple as we used to call it, without the risk of being tarnished by any of the natural legacy issues of Air Miles. Even the greenest of greenies out there would trust it and embrace it. From an eco-authenticity perspective, this would clearly be the preferred scenario. But by blending it all into one and adding as much green as possible into the DNA of the existing Air Miles program, we would be gaining something else of immense importance: much greater reach and scale of impact. With collector cards in almost three-quarters of all households in Canada, we could have a much more profound influence on consumer behaviour across the entire country from the very start simply by tilting the Air Miles program a little more in favour of the environment. After much debate, involving a lot of people from both original teams, we settled on full integration, and, since our focus was so obviously on maximizing our impact, I acquired one of the strangest business titles in the country: Air Miles' Chief Impact Officer.

We set out to prove that the naysayers and the cynics (and there were quite a few) had been wrong. I was adamant that I hadn't just sold my soul and my business to the devil of consumerism—I had simply managed to get my hands on the largest steering wheel, with an incredible ability to influence the direction and the behaviour of millions of consumers from coast to coast. If I had launched my original green points program, I would have had to start from influencing just one consumer, the very first one who would sign up for our points, and then the second, and the third and hopefully eventually the one-millionth. It would have been the purest and most wholesome loyalty points program on the planet, but it would have taken a long time for it to effect real change on a mass scale. This way, however, the only limit to our potential positive influence on the entire country was our own imagination and the extent to which we could tweak the Air Miles brand without affecting its existing mass appeal and power.

The first thing we did, before even touching the way Air Miles points worked for the average consumer, was to green the company. Nothing could neutralize cynics and critics better than real, hard evidence of our investment in becoming a corporate beacon of environmental inspiration for others. Air Miles was a recognized and visible brand, so there was an awesome opportunity for us to stand out from the large corporate crowd. Internally, we quickly rolled out some big sustainability ideas that were truly original and ignited excitement and passion among our fifteen hundred employees. We covered the large roof of our brand-new suburban call centre with so many solar panels that we instantly became the largest corporate solar energy producer in Canada. We installed a fleet of Smart cars under our corporate head-quarters tower in downtown Toronto, because we knew that many more of our employees would take public transit to work if they knew they could have access to a car during the day for meetings or errands. (Anyone could book out one of those cars, anytime, for any reason.) And we kept going down that creative path. We avoided doing the conventional stuff and focused on the more innovative ideas that would really inspire and would make us the talk of the town. It all came together beautifully, and the work was championed mostly by one of my former Green Rewards employees, who had blended quite effectively into Air Miles' much more conventional corporate culture and managed the internal methodical "selling" behind these new ideas.

My bigger job was to figure out how to change the way our coveted billions of miles touched consumers every day. We started with the easy stuff. We took a look at the Air Miles website, which was one of the busiest sites in the entire country. Millions of Canadians came to it every month, to check their balances, learn about the latest offers at their favourite stores or redeem their miles for a reward. With such a vast, loyal audience at our fingertips, why not tweak the site and turn it into a bit of an environmental guidepost? Why not gather content from some of the most trusted places in the country (the environmental NGOs, the government, even some of our giant retail partners), package it all up and then rebroadcast it to Canadians, almost like a free public service? It was such an easy thing to do, it cost us very little money, and it earned us amazing accolades from even the strictest environmentalists. We created the one spot online where Canadians could find aggregated, credible information on how to renovate their home, what kind of car they should be driving or the most environmentally responsible choices on offer at the grocery store.

Our next layer of work involved the essence of what we had been building back at Green Rewards: we gave Canadians a vast new range of much more eco-friendly rewards to choose from as they redeemed their miles. A lot of the core work had already been done by my old team, but armed with the heft and the name of Air Miles, we were able to expand on it dramatically. For example, in addition to offering all sorts of eco-merchandise to our millions of collectors, we talked to all the big public transit systems about buying monthly passes from them; soon Canadians were also able to redeem their miles for transit passes in most major cities across the country. And we hired one of the best-known environmental accreditation agencies in the country to help us screen and rate all those eco-rewards, so that consumers never needed to doubt the authenticity of what we put in front of them. It wasn't just us encouraging them to redeem their miles on some green product—it was a completely impartial third party endorsing those rewards and explaining why those particular products were a better choice for the planet.

The last and most critical part of program greening was to start rewarding Canadians with more miles when they shopped more responsibly. This was the toughest project, because it wasn't entirely within our control. We had to work hard to bring along all our big clients, some of whom were a lot bigger than us, and show them how doing this together with us would help their businesses and their brands. And we had to orchestrate it in a way that would create an influential and significant event for millions of consumers at once: we needed a lot of these big retailers to launch their eco-offers at the same time, to make the shift noticeable across the whole country.

It took us a whole year from the time the Green Rewards deal closed, but finally, in the fall of 2009, we went to market with a fantastic range of green bonus offers across Canada, together with our grocers, pharmacies, home improvement retailers, credit card issuers and others. It made a strong impact and, once again, made us the talk of the industry and of the broader media as well. For the first time anywhere in the world, consumers were earning extra loyalty points when they made environmental choices in their everyday lives; they earned bonus miles for buying organic or local food at the grocery store, wines with a lower carbon footprint at the liquor store, better paints and cleaning products for their homes, or even for switching from a paper credit card bill to an electronic one.

For me, that launch felt like the fulfillment of everything I had envisioned back on that day when I was sitting in my backyard wondering how to build something new around this emerging megatrend. In the span of two and a half years, I had chased the dream, built an audacious little disruptor business, sold it to the biggest possible buyer and infected that buyer with all the right stuff that ultimately led them to launch this whole thing (in remarkable scale) across the whole country. I remember the first time Joe and I saw one of those Air Miles commercials on TV about earning bonus miles with eco-purchases at a slew of retailers—I felt like crying. I think most kids grow up wanting to become inventors, and that night, for the first time ever, I realized that, against all odds and expectations, I had actually done it.

While we were all busy building and changing so much together, the media buzz that had started in our early days with Green Rewards continued to grow. It was still largely focused on me, as the original "inventor" and prime storyteller of the greening of Air Miles. The fact that I was no longer an entrepreneur and didn't really own any of this anymore didn't much matter to the journalists, who were drawn to my personal-disruption story. That was perhaps the start of a gradual buildup of tension and discomfort for me and towards me inside that much larger company. The media may have preferred to present it as the story of the irreverent, fearless disruptor, but the PR department of one of the country's most recognized and most cautious brands was not thrilled. It was tough to take the outspoken, impatient entrepreneur out of the boy—there were so many cool stories to tell, so many hungry journalists to charm, so many conference podiums looking for a spicy story. It often felt like I was dragging Air Miles behind me publicly every single day, and it also started to feel like that slow, cautious giant was less and less comfortable with the style and speed differential.

Just months after the acquisition I was invited to take part in a Canadian CEO roundtable on sustainability. The impressively high-profile group included the heads of banks, leading consumer brands, technology firms and environmental NGOs from across the country. At the end of our day together we would be joined by Prince Charles, who was in Toronto on an official visit, and we would be asked to share and debate our proposed solutions with him. At that time the prince was one of the most outspoken and prominent environmentalists in the world, and he was on a global search for big ideas with the potential to generate significant results. So when he joined us late that afternoon and we all began to introduce ourselves and talk about our particular stories and organizations, he immediately zeroed in on my story of shifting behaviours on a mass scale through a trickle of tiny, frequent rewards. I so clearly remember him pointing at me from across that huge table and then saying to all the other participants: "You all should find ways to impact the behaviour of the masses just like that gentleman is doing with his points program!" As if that wasn't enough to stun me, as he was leaving the room, he walked past my seat, gave me a light punch on the arm and said, "Do keep me posted on your progress, will you?"

My friend Gerry Butts, who at the time was running WWF-Canada and was sitting next to me when this happened, immediately turned to me and said, "Now that's an invitation to stay in touch with the palace, if I've ever heard one." And so I did, again to the bewilderment of my corporate communications colleagues. For the next twelve months, each time I sent a note and an update to the prince, I received a very warm reply. And then, totally unexpectedly, I received an invitation to visit him. He was hosting a group of senior corporate leaders from around the world to discuss a globally coordinated corporate strategy on climate change, and not only did he invite me to join that group (I was the most junior person in the room, by a mile), but he also asked if I could come prepared to discuss the possibility of transplanting my Canadian rewards idea to the U.K.

So off I went on another life first: an official visit to Clarence House, pinching myself every step of the way but also fully prepared to make the most of it. I was received by the head of the Prince's Charities, a remarkable man by the name of Sir Tom Shebbeare. Sir Tom appeared to have been briefed perfectly by His Royal Highness on my Canadian work and was exceptionally eager to charm me and to figure out with me how to set up a similar eco-rewards scheme in their country. He gave me a personal tour of Clarence House, the prince's official residence, and even walked me through the private quarters of the two younger princes, William and Harry, neither of whom were married yet, so they were both still living with their father. I remember when he pointed out Prince Harry's private parking spot in front of the door to his "apartment"— and how it all felt so unbelievable, as if I was immersed in a film.

We then settled in his office, along with his staff, and we proceeded to have a long discussion about transplanting my idea across the pond. I was dying to say yes, and I was struggling to come up with some sort of creative path, but I already knew that it would be impossible for us to pursue the idea. Nectar, the most popular points program in the U.K., was owned at the time by our fiercest global competitor, so the odds of my new masters back in Toronto having any appetite to collaborate with them in order to create a replica of our Canadian program were non-existent. The best I could offer Sir Tom was the possibility that someday, when my earn-out obligations to Air Miles expired and I was able to move on, perhaps we could look at doing something together. He understood, thanked me for my time, and then we both walked over to one of the main (enormous, impressive and stifling hot) reception lounges in the palace, where the prince was about to host the global leaders.

The self-pinching continued. I was sitting with some of the biggest corporate names in the world, watching as each of them would stand up so respectfully and pitch their powerful commitments to the persuasive and passionate prince. And there he was, singling me out once again and talking about the "brilliance" of our Canadian model that inspires millions of consumers to shift their behaviour positively, without any of the common guilt or punishment. And there it was again, that same hot flush on my cheeks that I had first experienced as a tiny first-grader on that balcony after my TV appearance—perhaps enhanced a bit by the sweltering heat in that room.

Even before we sold the business to LoyaltyOne, I had gotten to know Al Gore. When he began to train people around the world as his authorized message spreaders, I approached him about organizing a training session just for Canadian YPOers. The idea took a while to develop, and it was broadened along the way, but eventually I brought him together with a group of YPOers along with a significant number of my Green Rewards colleagues for his first-ever training session of Canadians, in Montreal in April 2008. That event made us the first-ever Canadian business with more than one Gore-trained staff member. It was a standout claim to fame for us, particularly back then when the whole climate change discussion was still more like a debate. Making several of my colleagues authorized spokespeople on behalf of Al Gore was somewhat of a big deal. It was the Gore training that launched me into public speaking.

While I was running around the country, and sometimes to Clarence House, the Palace, spreading our story and touting our accomplishments, a big surprise was brewing back in Toronto: an Ontario government department was contemplating using Air Miles as an incentive for people to conserve electricity. It was an idea that one of my brilliant former employees, before I sold the business, had once created, and he had infected some of his government contacts with it. Until then, the only two things governments could use to promote more responsible behaviour among citizens were advertising and cash incentives (rebates, coupons, discounts and so on). Advertising works, but it's not efficient or easily targeted and it's never easy to figure out how well it worked or who exactly has responded to a certain message. Cash incentives also work, but they're even less efficient and, once again, it's difficult to determine exactly where and how they may have made a real difference.

So my former colleague approached an energy conservation authority in Toronto and proposed to them that if they used loyalty points as an incentive, they would not only save a lot of money (because they would be rewarding only those whose behaviour truly changed) but also gain a much clearer understanding of who responded better to these types of offers. With this information, they could design programs that were even better targeted and more efficient. The idea had percolated a bit at the beginning, but it died when I sold the business to Air Miles and the conservation authority assumed that we were no longer authentic enough for them to work with. Gradually, however, their appetite came back. They watched us transform the whole Air Miles program in a very real way, they saw retailers offering miles to Canadians for shopping more responsibly and they started to think that perhaps it was worth giving that whole incentive concept a try after all.

So in the spring of 2010, just as I thought all my impact work at Air Miles was done, and just as I had started contemplating my future somewhere else, we found ourselves launching the world's first partnership between a loyalty points program and a government. It turned into an incredible success: we took that agency's numbers from about 20,000 participants in its conservation campaign in 2009 (through advertising) to more than 140,000 participants in

2010, while reducing the program's budget by a stunning two-thirds. We quickly realized we were on to something remarkable, so we rushed to set up a brand-new business under LoyaltyOne. We called it Air Miles for Social Change, and its only mission was to deploy miles as incentives, mostly in partnership with governments, and reward Canadians when they made eco-responsible lifestyle choices, from taking public transit to conserving electricity, to recycling, to diverting hazardous waste.

The opportunities were endless and the momentum was terrific. Our wild success with that first program in Ontario led to an avalanche of calls and conversations with potential partners all over the country, and there was a time, in the early part of 2011, when we could not keep up with the work. In every case, our results were spectacular. Sometimes things would go *too* well, and we would crash the websites of our government clients if a program required online participation (for instance, when we asked Canadians to participate in some type of awareness-building quiz or a pledge). In other cases, we would blow our clients' budgets in record time—because they hadn't anticipated so much public appetite and so many people to reward, and they would have to scramble to unlock more budget while programs were still running. But invariably, the results ranged from great to off the charts, and we were off on yet another exhilarating ride.

And then came an even bigger and sweeter surprise. Barely a year into our success with government partnerships on environmental incentives, we got a call from the B.C. Ministry of Health asking whether they could experiment with using loyalty points to encourage people to eat healthier. We had not seen this one coming, and I felt a bit embarrassed that we were being essentially out-innovated by a stodgy old government agency. At the same time, though, I was thrilled at the opportunity, and we threw ourselves at it with plenty of passion. In June 2011, we launched the world's first healthy-eating incentive program across the entire province of British Columbia, in partnership with the provincial government, the Heart and Stroke Foundation and the largest grocery chain in the Canadian west. Perhaps not surprisingly by this point, the results were stunning. We were able to make a clearly measurable and significant difference in the food choices people were making at the grocery store, just by dangling a few bonus miles in front of them.

That simple concept is anything but rocket science, and yet, once again, we happened to be the first people to ever try it anywhere in the world. And, just as had happened before, our initial success in British Columbia opened up the floodgates for us across the country and across every imaginable form of health promotion. Canadians were suddenly being offered miles to exercise, to join smoking cessation programs, to take an online health quiz or to engage with a health charity such as Heart & Stroke. The ride was even wilder this time, and by the middle of 2012, more than 70 per cent of our new business was coming from health-promotion programs. The same amazing Owen who had been with me since our humble early days at Green Rewards was now in charge of our health-promotion work, and his energy and passion were the biggest forces behind the explosive growth of that business.

As we became ever more entrenched in areas of public policy, I found myself developing some very interesting and rewarding relationships with big public policy thinkers. This was different from our early glamour days with the likes of Al Gore, David Suzuki and Prince Charles. In this new phase of our program, we were being invited to help develop transformative ideas for our nation along with politicians and senior public servants. I had always been fascinated by political and policy leadership but somehow never imagined myself being close to that world. Now, though, I was meeting mayors and premiers and ministers. The deputy premier of Ontario at the time, George Smitherman, who had once been skeptical of our ideas, became one of our most outspoken fans and, eventually, a good friend. David Collenette, one of the best-known elder statesmen on our federal political scene, also became a terrific supporter, a formal advisor and a great friend. And Justin Trudeau, who was introduced to me by my friend and former green collaborator Gerry Butts, quickly became a passionate partner in some of my public-speaking gigs and a friend who continues to inspire me to dream bigger and conform even less.

Here's how Justin and I first bonded. When I moved to Canada in the early 1980s, Justin Trudeau's dad, who was again prime minister at that time, was a powerful role model for me. I would watch him on TV and read about him and try to follow his thinking and his style. I wanted to grow up to be just like him—smart, edgy, funny, dismissive of fools, courageous and definitely quirky. Without knowing much about marketing and brand-building back then, I admired how he had been able to craft and maintain such a sharp and distinctive brand for himself. I was so fascinated by his leadership style that, when I grew a little older and became a bit more successful and connected, I tried to find ways to meet him.

By then he was a very old man, living in Montreal; all I wanted to do was to sit down with him and simply thank him for all the inspiration he inadvertently offered me as a young Canadian, and also thank him for the welcoming, cool, modern and inclusive society that was waiting for me here when I arrived. So I worked at this plan, talked to a few people who were connected with him, but just as I got close to making it happen, he died.

I was so upset on the day he died that I sat down and wrote him a letter. It was a short, cathartic note, ending with the line "*Au revoir*, dear teacher and friend I never met"—just a poor substitute for all the things I never got to say to him in person. That letter wasn't really meant to go anywhere—I just wrote it to make myself feel better as I was watching the news of his death, and then I put it away. But one day, when I happened to mention the story of the letter to my friend Gerry over lunch, he asked me to send it to him, and then he forwarded it to his best friend, Justin Trudeau. To my amazement, Justin called, said he wanted to thank me for the way that letter had made him feel and told me he wanted to come to Toronto and meet me. And the unlikeliest of friendships was hatched. (I've included the letter among the "Extras" at the end of this book.)

Back at work, Air Miles for Social Change had become our very own crazy little entrepreneurial venture inside the rigid corporate walls of our parent company, and it felt a lot like we were nurturing an accidental granddaughter of Green Rewards—same attitude, same appetite for risk and bold pronouncements, same client culture and definitely the same young energy. The crazier and faster we moved, the more obvious the contrast and the tensions with the much bigger shop that surrounded us. They were as big and comfortable and change-averse as we were wild, excitable, celebrated, unorthodox and energetic. We were building and winning new things, new types of clients and new types of programs, all of which required us to think in ways that were completely new for Air Miles; by contrast and largely by default, their culture had grown over many years to become quite safe and resistant to disruptive new ideas, styles and behaviours. Over time, perhaps quite naturally, the stable and superb profitability of the core Air Miles program had spawned a cautious and change-resistant culture, particularly among the leadership team—and my "tribe" of fast-moving, dreamy world-changers was becoming more and more of a nuisance. Not to mention my unfiltered, neuro-atypical style, which no doubt amplified the contrast and the jitters. Even Bryan was showing more signs of anxiety, no matter what his earlier pronouncements were about buying us to allow our entrepreneurial spirit to infect his team. Publicly he would always boast about the impact of Air Miles for Social Change, but privately he seemed increasingly uncomfortable with the kinds of buttons we were pushing.

The whole situation came to an abrupt boil when Bryan hired a very strange fellow to run his Air Miles business in Canada so he could shift his own focus to global opportunities. My new boss didn't appear to understand why my in-house social venture even existed or where it had come from, but he had apparently received clear permission to get rid of me (and the stand-alone social venture) if he didn't see a fit. And so he did, almost immediately, sparing my friend Bryan the discomfort of a face-to-face conversation with me. He walked into my office one morning and handed me a simple executive separation package. I felt surprised and relieved at the same time—but when I asked him how he intended to handle the balance of our earn-out agreement, he stared at me blankly and said, "What earn-out?" Visibly embarrassed, he asked me to give him an extra day to "get a better understanding of the situation." It was a comic scenario, for me at least.

An almost unbelievable string of missteps and miscalculations on their part kept deepening their self-inflicted crisis. Instead of offering a simple, logical path to resolving our earn-out agreement, the strange man came back the next day with a laughable suggestion that we should just keep that agreement in place for the remainder of its term, even with me gone from the job—essentially suggesting that Dean and I should simply trust him to continue running my business in my absence. It was such a naive offer, and we used it as fodder for a straightforward yet significant legal claim. With that one silly move, we could clearly demonstrate that the buyer was dealing with us in bad faith ("Get out of the way, let me run your old business any which way I want, and I will pay you based on how it performs").

The legal escalation drew in Bryan, even though he had tried so hard to avoid a direct confrontation with me by assigning the dirty work to his strange colleague. And, unsurprisingly—because the issue was so odd and the solution so obvious, so basic, it didn't take long for that whole standoff to be resolved correctly: the earn-out agreement was discontinued, Dean and I were paid fair value for the business, and my friendship with Bryan was permanently shattered. My dreamy young colleagues were gone shortly after that, and our social venture shrivelled rapidly and disappeared. The strange new fellow who had triggered this whole bizarre mess was also gone from Air Miles within a few months.

There was so much to reflect on. This was my first serious collision in the business world, and, oddly, I felt I had gained a lot more than fair compensation from it. It was complicated but deeply rewarding. I remember comparing it to how someone would feel if they had prevailed in an ugly custody battle over a child. It was my first-born that we had been battling over, and the intensity of my fight felt perfectly proportionate to the injustice. I was proud of my ability to confront so directly, and I was fascinated by Bryan's aversion to direct confrontation, which I had always found to be a common and troubling trait among mainstream corporate leaders. Was it my autism and my lack of filters that made me so blunt, stark and unrelenting in confronting others? Could it be that my neuro-atypical wiring was in fact a distinct entrepreneurial advantage? Is it perhaps a trainable skill for others?

More importantly, my newfound distance from the safe, cautious and predictable corporate world offered me a new perspective on how I really wasn't made for that world—or, perhaps more accurately, how that world really wasn't made for people like me. I was free again. I could create and build and drive once again, without all the cultural, structural and situational constraints of the previous few years at Air Miles. There was no PR department to frustrate with my insatiable appetite for making noise, no HR department to frighten with my intensity and insufficient filters. I was back to charting my own twisted and fun path through life, enriched with even more confidence and with the spoils of my first-ever true "exit" as an entrepreneur.

The only real casualty of that crisis was my friendship with Bryan. Initially I was remorseful about that and kept second-guessing my decision—or instinct—to fight as hard as I had, but he then continued to behave in a way that erased that remorse and made me feel fully vindicated. His public bitterness towards me escalated into a spectacular faux pas a few years later, right when I was proudly launching my next business (more on this later). On reflection, I felt incredibly relieved when he made that final misstep, because it gave me the evidence I needed that there never had been a friendship worth mourning or resurrecting. What a more neuro-typical person would have easily identified from the start as a purely transactional and perhaps even opportunistic relationship had obviously been overestimated in my atypical mind, just the way I had misread and overvalued so many other human connections since I was a little kid—and that's the only reason I had struggled to understand his behaviour through our separation.

CARROT

ON A DREARY OTTAWA AFTERNOON, deep inside a quiet and cozy sushi restaurant, my heart was racing as I listened to my lunch guest. His name was Rodney Ghali, and he was a soft-spoken, gentle senior public servant in our federal government. I had known Rodney from the days when I was running Air Miles for Social Change—he was the visionary at the Public Health Agency of Canada who had spotted an opportunity to work with us by using smart incentives to get people to be more physically active. That particular program, which was truly a first of its kind in the world, had been a perfect multi-sector partnership: the federal government, the YMCA (where we would send Canadians to exercise), the Heart and Stroke Foundation and us, the incentives provider. The results had been exceptional, and all the contributors to the original idea—none more than Rodney and myself—had felt proud of ourselves for the difference we had made in society in such a simple way.

Sadly, that first physical-activity rewards program wasn't followed by anything else because that was the very last thing we built before my exit from Air Miles and the collapse of our social venture. For a couple of years after that, I was restrained by the typical post-sale legal shackles that are designed to prevent entrepreneurs from returning and potentially messing up the lives of the buyers of their previous businesses. It had felt like everything around me, the good ideas and the good people with them, had all been put on hold for all that time, waiting for the clock to strike two years from my corporate divorce. We kept talking about and celebrating the past successes, but nobody dared get to work on the natural next thing. It seemed everyone was waiting for me to say it was okay to dream and invent again.

I had filled the air and the time with hints and speculation. I wasted no time in setting up a new company, named it Social Change Rewards (a cheeky blend of the names of my previous two businesses) and focused it exactly on their footsteps, but just not in Canada. I latched on to that old request by Prince Charles and wrapped a complete business plan around it: a wellness rewards program for the U.K., offering all citizens their choice of their most favourite and popular everyday loyalty points for living healthier lives. I was riding on the awesome credibility of all our previous successes in Canada.

My co-founders and I, all of us Canadians, would be launching a Canadian-headquartered business to operate entirely in another country. Nobody believed us, not even the British journalists who came to our business unveiling at Canada House, in London, in the spring of 2013. "Why do this here, when all your credibility and momentum stems from Canada?" was their first, perfectly natural question. The concept of offering a choice of popular rewards, to maximize appeal and relevance across the entire population, was so obvious, so logical and—on the heels of all our successes with Air Miles—so Canadian. And yet here we were, clearly running out the clock on my legal restrictions back home.

At some point, exasperated and excited by all the momentum that was building even back home from the echoes of our U.K. story, we approached Bryan and his team at Air Miles and tried to get them to consider lifting the legal restrictions, to allow us to launch in Canada first. We explained how our new, currency-agnostic platform idea would actually be good for Air Miles and would bring them more business. Their loyalty program was the most popular in Canada at the time, so if we could launch and include theirs as a leading reward currency, they would instantly capture a huge slice of the pie and would be issuing many more miles (not to mention the positive association for their brand). It all made so much sense. But the air was still full of bitterness, and their response was a flat "no."

As it turns out, a much bigger twist in life ended up filling the time that was left on that legal clock. In the spring of 2014, with absolutely no warning, Joe suffered a heart attack. It happened when I was flying back from a speech in Greece and it marked the beginning of the most frightening and destabilizing two months in our lives. The heart attack, of course, got us to the hospital, where something much more severe happened while he was being monitored and prepped for a procedure: he died for a very long minute. His heart stopped for sixty seconds, the hospital was reverberating with "code blue" commands over the PA system, and we discovered that my beautiful partner had been born with a seriously defective heart and was incredibly lucky to have survived until the age of forty-nine. His condition is called heart block—an extreme form of arrhythmia that, in certain situations, causes a heart to simply stop beating. For some people the very first episode of that can be fatal—their heart would never restart. For the luckier ones it does restart, although it's impossible to predict how many episodes a person can survive.

In Joe's case, once we were able to stitch together the stories going all the way back to when he was a baby, it appears that he had always suffered these heart-stopping episodes, they were always quite long (much longer than a few seconds) and they were consistently misdiagnosed as bizarre fainting events. Joe's dad and sisters had a tendency to pass out, so over the years everyone (including me) came to assume that Joe was also just a frequent fainter. None of us ever thought to check his pulse while he was lying unconscious on so many occasions, over so many years—simply because none of us ever suspected it could have been anything that severe. It would happen more commonly in low-oxygen or high-altitude settings, such as airplanes, and we would both get frustrated by the inconvenience and the embarrassment of medical emergencies onboard, but we never imagined how close to the edge we got every single one of those times. It was also easier for his heart to stop when he was very tired, so that was likely what triggered the episode at the hospital after his heart attack—he was exhausted after spending the night in a busy emergency ward, and he even told me that he felt he was going to pass out, so in fact I had left our room to go look for a nurse when the episode began. His heart monitor triggered the "code blue" alarm, which I assumed was coming from someone else.

When I casually strolled back into our room, I found a half-dozen doctors and nurses over him, screaming commands at each other, ready to resuscitate him—and then suddenly his heart restarted by itself, as it had always done in the past, and he slowly began to regain consciousness. In that mayhem, I tapped one of the doctors on the shoulder and tried to calm him down by telling him that this happened to us all the time. The doctor turned to me, stunned. "What happens all the time, sir?" he said. I pointed at Joe: "This—he passes out frequently." To which the now visibly agitated doctor replied: "Sir, do you have any idea what just happened to your spouse?" And he pointed to the monitor above the bed, which showed an absolute flatline for the previous sixty seconds. I couldn't process it. I saw Joe's beautiful face, contorting with discomfort as he slowly returned to consciousness, and I just couldn't understand how I had almost lost him—so many times.

Our life was turned upside down. Now the only thing that mattered was that tiny, overstretched thread that Joe's life was hanging from—the relatively minor heart attack that had brought us to the hospital was a blessing in disguise, because it had exposed that tiny thread for us. We were devastated, but we also felt incredibly lucky. Joe could have died from any one of those episodes that had started when he was still in the crib. Within days, our mood had shifted from shock and fear to gratitude. We were so grateful for the way things had turned out, grateful that he had survived his episodes before that accidental diagnosis, grateful for the love we both had for life and for each other. He was quickly "repaired"—all it took was an awesome, tiny pacemaker—and he went back to work after a couple of weeks.

But then, just a couple of weeks after Joe came home from the hospital, bam—a second, unbelievable hit: cancer, in me. Once again, it took a good deal of luck (my noticing a tiny bit of blood in my urine) to trigger a terrifying diagnosis of advanced and aggressive bladder cancer. Back to the same hospital we went, back to the OR, back through the same extreme rollercoaster of emotions. And back to the same happy ending—fully "repaired," filled with just as much gratitude and love as the first time.

I came out of those two existential scares feeling almost reborn. There were new perspectives on everything—every day, every human relationship, every notion of success and wealth and purpose in life. Everything felt completely and crisply redefined for me. My pervasive, uncontrollable irreverence went from something I was trying to squish or hide to something that proudly defined me. I was finally aware of how short life can be. Instead of paralyzing me, all the drama of 2014 became my rocket fuel. It gave me a whole new layer of fearlessness and impatience. I felt so much more ready to create, change and conquer. And I was so happy that, in the meantime, the legal clock had advanced much closer to midnight.

By the time the shackles were gone and I met Rodney for that fateful chat in Ottawa, the momentum behind our new business idea was tremendous and the path towards a Canadian launch seemed short and perfectly clear to both of us. We sat at that restaurant for what seemed like hours, imagining something so different and so effective for nudging millions of people to live better. "Nudge" theory was spreading around the world at that time, and we both wanted our new concept to quickly become the celebrated approach in that new space. We decided to go mobile only—reach and influence people just through their phones, with a very simple, friendly, fun and rewarding mobile app. We'd be harnessing two of the most intense social habits of our fellow citizens—the overwhelming attachment to our smartphones and our national addiction to collecting points.

A few weeks later, on a flight back from another speech, this time in Mexico City, I was reviewing our official proposal to partner with the Public Health Agency of Canada. My awesome young co-founder Jordan, who had worked with me in my last business, had patiently authored our seventy-page submission to the government, explaining exactly why the country needed this sort of wellness rewards platform, why we were the most qualified experts to build it and how we would work with the feds to launch it, populate it and turn it into a unique success story and a world beacon. It took the entire five-hour flight for me to leaf through it all, and I remember walking out of that plane filled with an interesting new blend of emotions—the same unconditional excitement I had felt when Dean and I were starting Green Rewards almost a decade earlier, but this time a good deal of intimidation was hanging over me. Green Rewards had once been a wild, bold idea with no precedent and no real expectations around it. This new thing was also wild and bold and a first of its kind in the world, but its effective "co-founder" was going to be the Government of Canada—and that, in my head at least, meant that it came with an absolute heap of expectations. It had to work. It had to make a difference. It had to stand out. And it had to be huge.

Our seventy-page tome began to work its way through the complex approval processes of government. Rodney and his team were passionately committed to guiding the process, and all we could do was trust them and wait. And then came another special homeward-bound-flight moment: on the sixteenth of January, 2015, as Joe and I were about to board the plane back to Toronto from a quick vacation in Costa Rica, I got an email from Rodney, asking if we could chat by phone a couple of hours later. I suggested we delay till that evening because I would be in the air for most of the day, and he wrote back right away, with this: "Congratulations, my friend: our program and funding has been approved by the Minister of Health. I wanted to tell you by phone and savour your reaction, but I really don't think I could wait until tonight!"

I will never forget that flight home. Joe raised a glass and proudly said, "You're back!" And I felt it. I was filled with awesome new fuel, enriched with so much more perspective, riding the biggest credibility wave of my crazy career and surrounded by believers. It was time for the big time.

A week or two later I was judging the presentations of MBA students in the entrepreneurship stream at Ivey, one of the top-rated business schools in our country. I had served as a coach and a judge in that program for years and had always enjoyed the experience. I learned so much from being involved and loved the way it stretched me, almost beyond my comfort zone, to have some of the smartest and most ambitious business minds in the country as my "students" for a short while each year. That particular day, however, something extraordinary happened. One of the teams I was judging showed up with a presentation that looked like a partial version of my brand-new wellness rewards business. They were pitching a social venture that would help reduce texting while driving with an approach very similar to ours—tiny nudges in the form of a stream of rewards. As if that wasn't enough to grab my attention, the leader of the group was a superbly eloquent, sharp, confident, truly charismatic presenter. At the end of the session I called her over, introduced myself, told her a few things about the national platform I was about to build and suggested we catch up very soon. She eagerly agreed.

That same evening, on my long drive to Toronto, I got a call from an old friend from YPO, Elizabeth Frank. Elizabeth had been a mainstream corporate executive for her entire career and recently and prematurely had retired after spending more than twenty years in the same company. She was hungry for a new project, and she was thinking about plunging into something a lot more entrepreneurial, so we had started chatting a few weeks earlier about my new business. From the very start I had wanted to get someone else to run the company. I kept declaring that I never wanted another job per se—I wanted to create this new venture, nurture it, give it lots of momentum, but trust a much more conventional hands-on operator to pull it all together for the long term. Our phone call that evening ended up becoming the "yes" moment for both of us. We compared our enormous differences and our completely non-overlapping leadership styles, but we also both found ourselves getting swept up by the optimism that swirled around the birth of my new project. With an official mandate from the federal government and a clear path forward, it felt safe enough for Elizabeth—we had more than enough of a foundation to attract investors, and that gave her the comfort to jump in as the first employee.

When Sarah Richard, the impressive young woman from Ivey, came to Toronto to have that chat with me, she found Elizabeth by my side, and that probably made it a tiny bit easier for her to say yes and join our crazy show as well. None of us knew what each specific role would look like, but we were all joining hands and agreeing to row together. Sarah joined us the moment she finished her MBA, and she's been by my side ever since, eventually becoming our chief product officer.

Then came Marc Mitchell, the kindest genius and humblest health/nudge expert in our country. I met him as he was finishing his PhD in a field that was the absolute epicentre of my new world: the intersection of public health and incentives. I was giving a speech in Ottawa about how we were going to build this unique wellness rewards platform and I found myself having to answer a stream of questions posed by the ultimate Canadian expert in the field. When I finally stepped off the podium and asked my hosts about the man whose hand had kept going up, they all seemed surprised that I didn't know who Marc Mitchell was. And, just as with Sarah at Ivey, Marc and I were immediately intrigued by our overlapping ideas and passions, and he also ended up joining my founding team. He's been leading our behavioural insights ("nudge") work since the beginning.

Perhaps most intriguing of the senior founding colleagues was Matt. He wasn't new to my life—I had known him since he was a kid, when I used to work with his dad at Maritz. Joe and I had stayed friends with his parents, and I had developed a bit of a mentorship bond with Matt over the years. By his early thirties he had developed a cool career and reputation, primarily in the technology world, as a sophisticated business developer. His dad had been one of our most incredible sales geniuses at Maritz, and those awesome genes had certainly been passed on to Matt. He had blossomed into an eloquent networker, a global citizen and a hungry, quick, eager builder of ideas. Without knowing anything about my crazy new venture, he invited me out to drinks one evening for a bit of mentoring. I had never thought about working with him before, but our conversation and the way he understood and responded to my new business idea instantly sparked the thought: Could he be the sales leader we had been looking for? We were close to offering the job to someone else, so there was no time for a soft approach. I immediately mentioned the idea to him, his eyes lit up, I set him up to quickly do the rounds with my tiny early team, and within a few days we had stopped the presses on that other hire and Matt had joined our zoo with a mission to build a sales team and strategy.

The core leadership team was now in place. We kept adding more and more young, distinctive, passionate people as quickly as we found them. Some would not even join us for a specific job or because they had specific skills—we would simply bring them in because we liked who they were and how they thought. There certainly was no shortage of work, right from the start, but there was a distinct shortage of structure and job descriptions. We were all just building and creating, all the time, without trying to manage boundaries between roles. I remember one day when Megan, our youngest employee at the time, happened to be going to Ottawa with her mom for an extended weekend and offered to pop by one of our government clients' offices to give an in-person presentation of our program and plans (instead of having our team present by conference call). The offer was so generous and genuine on Megan's part, and we were all so fluid and risk-happy, that none of us objected. We went ahead and sent a brand-new twenty-three-year-old employee to give a critical in-person presentation to the country's financial literacy leader and her team. While our clients were blown away by what turned out to be an outstanding presentation, the rest of us back in the shop didn't even consider any of this to be extraordinary.

To support the rapid build, I needed to find investors as fast as possible—and I clearly had learned little about that part of the job, based on how unusual and almost accidental my arrangement with Dean had been in my previous business. I truly didn't know where to begin, so I asked my trusted friend and investor expert Adam to have dinner with me and help coach me. We met at my favourite Italian restaurant one evening and started to talk about how to structure the pitch and how to tell the story of where this business came from and what it could become. And the more we talked about it, the more Adam seemed to be derailed. Instead of structuring an investor pitch, he seemed to be convincing himself that he should be the first investor! By the end of our dinner I had another Dean-like situation—Adam was committing to personally lead my first investor round and build the first iteration of the company's board of directors. It was almost unbelievable.

Another critical piece was figuring out what to call this platform. It was going to be a mobile app and, if it was to be relevant and meaningful for millions of people, it needed to be branded very carefully. We assembled a team of experts at an agency to help pull this together, but then I showed up and immediately messed up their work with a quirky idea. A couple of years earlier, when all of this was still at fantasy stage, I had the good fortune of meeting Joe Clark, who had been our country's youngest prime minister for a brief time in 1979–80. Joe was intrigued by my work and asked me out to breakfast. And when I described to him the new idea of creating a national rewards platform to promote wellness, he glanced at me over his reading glasses and said, with the tone of a serious instructor, "Young man, carrots always work better than sticks."

The line remained etched in my mind, and when we brought together the brand-naming experts, I violated every bit of protocol by marching into the room charged with passion for the name I wanted: Carrot! I had already been reprimanded by my own Joe at home, who not only thought it would be inappropriate for me to interfere with the professionals in such an overt way, but was also convinced that the name Carrot would be a total flop. He thought consumers would feel manipulated by the obvious carrot-versus-stick connotation and he really wanted me to keep my mouth shut and let the pros do their work. Well, guess who just couldn't obey his spouse in that particular case—and we're all so glad for that now.

The pros were immediately enamoured with the suggestion and found absolutely no show-stoppers as they tested it. Carrot it was. The double entendre of the healthy vegetable and the incentive quickly made us such a simple, clear, memorable brand in everyone's eyes. And that turned out to be one of the rare occasions where my Joe was wrong.

Up next: convincing some of the largest points programs in our country to take us seriously and agree to sell us their points, so that Canadians could have choices of rewards on the Carrot app. We were tiny, and we were still just a promise and a theory; they were all huge, and they were used to doing huge deals with huge brands. Most start-ups scramble to find clients; we already had clients, who in fact were almost behaving as our co-founders, but we knew we would have to struggle to sign up our key suppliers. Without them, Carrot would simply not exist.

We quickly determined that the best way to gain some momentum in our conversations with those huge national points programs was by boosting our profile. If the national media published stories about us, then we would suddenly be credible and we would be taken a little more seriously. We spoke with Rodney in Ottawa about organizing a press event where the federal government would officially announce the birth of Carrot—and he immediately agreed. But the plan became complicated right away, because a public announcement would also need to involve the government of British Columbia, the province where Carrot would first be made available to consumers. We spent many weeks in the spring and summer of 2015 trying to line up the calendars of a federal and a provincial minister of health, along with the CEOs of all the national health charities that were involved in creating Carrot. We were all getting frustrated by how long this endless juggling was taking. It was slowing down our hunt for the most important thing we were missing: suppliers!

And then, one day in late July, I received an urgent message from Rodney, who had just heard rumours that the prime minister was about to call an early election. This would mean the government would dissolve, making it impossible for us to organize an announcement of any kind until long after the election and after the next cabinet was formed. Rodney and I agreed to immediately draft our joint press release, get it approved by his minister and by the B.C. health minister, and have us host the media event in Toronto on our own, without trying to get any politicians to join in person anymore. If we couldn't get this done ahead of the election call, we would easily lose several months from our launch plan. So the choice was already made for us, and in truly record time for all involved, press releases were written and approved, media were invited, and Carrot was formally announced by the Government of Canada on July 30, 2015, at a hastily organized press conference at the grand old YMCA facility in downtown Toronto, without a single government official in the room.

The election call and the dissolution of the government came just four days later. The whole situation reminded me of the close call with the sale of Green Rewards to Air Miles just days before the financial collapse of 2008.

Armed with national publicity, we thought we would have an easier time bringing onboard some of the most popular loyalty programs in the country. There was already a cheer-leader among them—the Scene movie rewards program, led by a brilliant modern thinker who immediately saw the ben-efits and the value of fuelling a national wellness platform, had agreed to be our first points supplier. We had invited the leaders of the top ten points programs to a briefing session, co-hosted by us and the Public Health Agency of Canada, and that's when I first met Matthew Seagrim, the general manager of Scene, and saw how passionate he was about join-ing. Several other rewards programs seemed interested, but it was soon obvious they were also more cautious. The two big-gest players in the country—Loblaw, with their ultra-popular grocery and pharmacy reward program, and my old pals at

Air Miles—both asked us for information and at first made it look like they would talk with the federal government. But both soon became public opponents of the Carrot program.

Giant Loblaw simply couldn't bring themselves to be just one of several players in a government-backed national platform. They understood the emerging national mood shift towards promoting wellness and they clearly wanted to ride the wave, but they already viewed themselves as the de facto national platform for influencing the behaviour of Canadians. If they did participate in something like Carrot, they would want it to be much more Loblaw-centric than the flat, democratic choice program we had so carefully designed with the federal government. At one point during our many exchanges they came right out and declared that the only way they could ever play would be if they owned a substantial part of the platform, if not the business itself. We tried, and our friends in the government tried even harder, but we just couldn't get them to budge. As much as we would have loved to boost the success of Carrot with the popularity of Loblaw's rewards—they claimed to have twenty million members in our small country of just thirty-six million souls—we realized we would have to do this without them.

The best part of that pursuit, however, was its humorous ending. More than a year after we launched, by which time our success and public impact were being celebrated everywhere, I happened to meet the family scion of the giant Loblaw business, Galen Weston Jr., at a political fundraiser in the summer of 2017. As soon as a mutual friend introduced us, Galen commended me effusively on our great work, as he described it, in changing the behaviour of an entire nation. I was stunned, and I immediately pounced. I said something along the lines of "Well, I'm so happy you feel that way, Galen, and even though we're so far along now and so established with all the other reward options for Canadians, it would still be wonderful to have you join our platform." To which, incredibly, he responded with the broadest smile and a line that I will never forget: "Andreas, it will never happen." I was speechless. It was impossible to compute the contradiction between his giant friendly smile and those words. I struggled to respond and all I came up with was a pathetic-sounding, "But why?" He responded, "Because we're building an even better version of a national wellness platform ourselves." By the time Joe and I had gotten back into our car, we were already giggling about that bizarre exchange. None of it felt crushing, the way a blunt rejection like this would have felt back when we were building my dream; it just felt entertaining, and empowering. In the midst of our giggles we looked at each other and we both confidently said that the only thing that could never happen was Loblaw being able to build a better or bigger version of Carrot.

And then there was Air Miles. They had clearly seen this coming—particularly when we had so explicitly asked them a year earlier to let us launch early in Canada and they had declined. Despite the past divorce and Bryan's obvious lingering bitterness towards me, we still really wanted them to join the coalition and benefit from the Carrot program. After all, every one of the great original examples of using rewards to promote wellness had their name on it, and it would look odd if they weren't part of the bigger and more permanent manifestation of everything we had created together when I was there. We invited them to the joint briefing with our government partners; they confirmed their plans to attend and even asked for the information package in advance. But then they didn't show up. We were disappointed but not overly fussed by their unexplained absence—until their next, truly shocking move.

Not even a week after the briefing, using information taken from our package, they sent out two letters. The first was to me, warning me not to proceed with the launch of Carrot because, even though our legal-restriction period was over, they claimed I was basing our business plans on proprietary and confidential knowledge I had gleaned while running Air Miles for Social Change; the letter was long, yet contained no specifics, not even a specific threat of remedial action, so it was obviously just a scare tactic. But their other letter went out to the CEOs of all the organizations who had attended the Carrot briefing—attaching a copy of the letter they had sent to me and very clearly trying to scare them away from participating in the Carrot coalition.

Few times in my life have I felt as livid or as crushed about my previous false perceptions as I felt that day about Bryan. It was such an intense throwback to my childhood days of painful disillusionment about others, when this chronically unfiltered kid would constantly fall into the same pothole of trusting unconditionally. It hurt to see such clear evidence that there had never been an ounce of genuine friendship with that man. But at the same time, my mix of pride and frustration instantly turned into determination to push back, and hard. Our lawyers were confident that we had a solid case against Air Miles for intentionally and unjustifiably interfering with our business, and we immediately pursued it. Consensus among all my investors at that point was that if we didn't sue right away, there was a real risk that our soon-to-be Carrot partners could be spooked— and the scare tactics by Air Miles could continue. I called our government partners in Ottawa to let them know, as a courtesy, that we were starting legal proceedings against Air Miles, and they, very wisely, asked us to hold off for a day or two while they tried to intervene directly with Bryan. And so they did—initially he didn't return their calls, but eventually Rodney managed to get hold of him, expressed his strong disappointment over that pointless and vendetta-like interference, and asked Bryan to back off. And so he did. That was the last we heard from Air Miles. And, of course, Carrot went on to launch and succeed without the participation of the most popular rewards program in the country.

It took us much longer than we had ever imagined to stitch together the initial coalition of suppliers of loyalty points. That hunt turned into an existential threat to the survival of our dream. It was proving a lot easier to get money, clients, supporters, media coverage and employees than it was to find those who wanted to take our money! It was that same old feeling from the days of building Green Rewards—while it was gratifying to be the tiny disruptor in a space of giants, the slightest sneeze by those giants could have proved fatal for us. In order for Carrot to make sense as a national behaviour-influencing platform, we needed to offer a good mix of reward options for Canadians; having only one or two points programs to choose from wouldn't cut it. In the end, we settled on having four initial partners for our launch: our outstanding and creative movie-reward friends at Scene, the country's main frequent flyer program (Aeroplan), a prominent gas rewards program (Petro-Points) and a grocery rewards program from western Canada (More Rewards). The balance and variety between the four were ideal—something for everyone, whether young, old, male, female, urban, suburban, rural, wealthy, lower income, etc.

By the time it all came together, we were exhausted, but we felt so proud of ourselves and we were ready to push forward with the launch. Just before Christmas 2015 we held a final gathering of our entire budding ecosystem: our four suppliers, our three national health charity partners, and the federal government as well as the government of British Columbia. We all joined hands on a firm plan to launch the app a few weeks later. It was the perfect capping moment for what had definitely felt like the most remarkable year in my career. A year earlier I had no employees, no clients, no suppliers, no investors and no technology—and here I was, wrapping up 2015 with more than a dozen fellow dreamers in the company, a gorgeous app ready to launch, layers of government contracts, investors, money in the bank and multiple suppliers and other national partner organizations.

The new year began with a few more doses of entrepreneurial thrills, commonly mislabelled "challenges." Our launch date on the West Coast kept slipping because, yet again, it was proving so hard to coordinate the calendars of various government folks. We had talked about launching early in January, to coincide with New Year's resolutions and the common desire to live better after the lazy holidays. We got delayed to the end of January, then again to the middle of February, and then a third time to the beginning of March. We were all frustrated, even our keen friends in the B.C. government, but we really couldn't do much about it—every calendar ultimately had to line up so that all the official contributors to our beautiful Carrot could be there to tell their story in front of the media. A few delays of a few weeks each time may have not seemed like a big deal to all our large partners, especially the government agencies, but I could see my young, fast-moving and passionate colleagues growing exasperated. I would get swept up in their impatience and would spread the stress by sometimes angrily echoing it all, in my own unfiltered and unrefined way, to our clients and partners. Eventually we all came up with a definite launch date: the third of March, 2016.

One of the least erasable visual memories of my career is from the basement of the magnificent British Columbia Parliament Buildings, in Victoria, on that launch day. Sarah and I were sitting next to each other in a dark corner of the staff cafeteria, where she was trying to get a bit of signal to connect back to our office while I was prepping my media remarks for later that morning. We planned to launch our app about an hour ahead of the press conference, hoping to have some real activity to report by the time I stood in front of the media. Right at 9 a.m., one of our partners, Scene, pushed out a big email blast to their members in British Columbia, offering them points for downloading this cool, free new wellness app called Carrot. At 9:01 a.m. Sarah checked our server stats to see if we'd had any downloads yet—and the answer was no. But when she checked again a couple of minutes later, she turned to me with a look of disbelief, pointing at her screen and almost screaming: "Look at this—240 new users!" Less than a minute later, she refreshed her screen and saw that we had more than three hundred users, and a few minutes later it was five hundred, and then seven hundred, a thousand . . . By the time I joined the provincial and federal health ministers in the green room before the mid-morning press conference, we were already closing in on two thousand users. I practically danced my way into that room, beaming and buzzing with the greatest numerical enthusiasm of my whole numerically obsessed life, even infecting both government ministers with it.

We marched out to the main atrium where the press conference was being staged, and I most impatiently waited for my turn on the podium, where I was going to be the final speaker. As the B.C. minister of health, Terry Lake, introduced me, he told the audience that I was going to reveal a happy surprise—and then I grabbed the mic, smiled proudly at everyone and said, "Ladies and gentlemen, our beautiful Carrot app went live in British Columbia a little over an hour ago, and I'm proud to share with you that, based on the latest data that's trickling in, we already have . . ."—and just as I was about to say two thousand users, I saw Sarah at the very back of the room waving frantically at me and then pointing at four fingers on her right hand. "Four thousand users," I finished. One in every thousand British Columbians had downloaded our app in the first hour after it became available. Our naive projection for the entire first year had been about thirty thousand downloads, and we ended up hitting that number within the first two days. Those kinds of moments are the stuff of every entrepreneur's fantasies. And they kept coming.

We quickly became conditioned to expect more and more excitement as we kept launching different offers across the country. We had definitely struck a chord with the creation of a simple, free, friendly app that gave out everyone's favourite loyalty points just for, really, paying attention to it! We crashed clients' servers; we crushed their budgets; we found ourselves in scenarios where clients were asking us to slow things down; and we had a tough time dealing with reality in those very few cases where our programs performed only as well as we expected. Overachievement became the Carrot norm in the first two years, and we all became quite happily drunk with that success.

Speaking of happiness . . . The province of Newfoundland and Labrador was lined up to be our next launch, just three months after B.C. The set-up and timing were going to be similar: a mid-morning press conference together with our government partners, right around the time when Newfoundlanders would start receiving emails about Carrot from their favourite points programs. Matt, who was leading all our government partnerships, flew out to St. John's with me the evening before. We were both picked up at the airport by Steve Kent, the former deputy premier and health minister who had approved the launch of Carrot in his province shortly before his party lost an election. Steve had quickly become a friend of ours, and even though he wasn't going to be formally involved in the following day's festivities, he definitely considered himself the proud instigator of what we all expected to be another Carrot adoption success.

Not at all surprisingly, Steve "ordered" us to simply drop off our bags at the hotel and then dragged us out to a typical night filled with Newfoundlander hospitality, warmth, endless singing and significant drinking. We started with the "screeching in" of Matt (who had never before endured that local custom), and then we hopped from one live music bar to another. Around two in the morning, Matt tried to convince us to end the festivities because we had to get a good night's rest before the next morning's media event. I looked at Steve through the fog of a serious number of drinks and we both laughed and told Matt to shut up and keep on drinking. He tried a second and a third time— and then, with a much more stern tone and a severe look on his face, he declared that he was leaving and that I better follow him back to the hotel.

I did not. Steve and I went on for quite a while longer and then we topped up our night of adolescent-like irresponsibility by searching the town for bad food, as a hopeless antidote to the damage of the previous several hours. Dawn was breaking over St. John's by the time I found my hotel room.

And, of course, I was shocked when I faced myself in the mirror a few hours later as I was trying to make myself presentable for the television cameras. The worst part was, I had absolutely no voice. Matt met me in the breakfast area with a honey-filled cup of tea and we managed to repair some of the damage, but I certainly didn't recognize my own voice by the time I greeted the crowd from the podium. I sounded like a superbly sexy baritone version of myself. It made sense to pre-empt any questions or gossip by dealing with the "issue" head-on in my opening remarks. There were endless giggles among the audience when I began by announcing that the only reason I sounded so sexy and so deeply male was because I had been very obedient when I was told to enjoy a significant dose of Newfoundlander warmth and hospitality immediately after landing in town the previous evening.

Our launch in that province was just as spectacularly successful as the one in British Columbia three months earlier. An almost unbelievable number of Newfoundlanders were using our app by the time we hosted another media gathering in St. John's to celebrate our one-year anniversary. The premier himself spoke at that event and proudly shared how Carrot had changed his life.

We initially launched Carrot as a pure wellness education app, serving our users a stream of informational quizzes designed to gently nudge them to learn how to live healthier. The quizzes were created by our team of behavioural scientists and public health specialists and were mostly based on information that was passed on to us by our government partners. Essentially, we took conventional (and often un-inspiring) government health campaigns and turned them into fun and engaging quizzes—and then we added rewards on top of that, which meant that Canadians were devouring those quizzes in numbers we had never even imagined. When we were designing the platform, we courageously guesstimated that the average user would complete 10 per cent of the quizzes we served them—and some considered that to be a wildly optimistic projection (especially given that the "conversion rate" of online or mass media advertising is typically no more than 1 per cent).

We felt quite confident, though, that rewards would make a huge difference in our app, compared with anything else that had been tried before, but we really had no idea how sticky and engaging a platform we were about to launch. When we saw the astronomical 83 per cent completion rate on the more than one hundred thousand quizzes we had pushed out on our first day in B.C., we thought it was either wrong data or a ridiculous fluke. We sobered up a bit when our second-day completion rate was again 83 per cent. And the same on the third and fourth and every day after that. We were rubbing our eyes and trying to calm down our stunned government clients whose money was flying out the door so much faster than anyone could have predicted.

But then, feeling inspired by the wild success of the quiz-zes and hungry to build on it, we decided to add to our app something even more radical and engaging and with an even more direct impact: rewards for walking each day. Because our app "lives" on people's smartphones and because almost all phones contain accelerometers that count users' daily steps, we thought it would make plenty of sense to create a trickle of rewards on Carrot to encourage people to achieve their daily step goal. We set each user's goal based on her or his historical daily steps average, to make it completely personalized and attainable, and we turned it on about three months after launching Carrot. The results were absolutely staggering. Within just weeks we started seeing a significant upward trend line, particularly among less physically active users. Within months we were able to start publishing peer-reviewed studies that showed dramatic increases in the daily physical activity of our (by then huge) population of Canadian users. Overall, we were able to push up the average daily steps of our many hundreds of thousands of users by 20 per cent—and those increases were even more spectacular among the half of the population who would have been considered sedentary.

With our quizzes we knew we were steadily influencing the attitudes of Canadians and increasing their health awareness, but with our steps rewards we were able to create and measure immediate and dramatic changes in behaviour on a mass scale. Nothing could have reinforced our pride in our work more than this evidence of the effect we were having on people's everyday lives. Not to mention the unprecedented and indescribable "nutritional value" of all those mountains of data for my numbers-ravenous mind. Being able to study behavioural outcomes across so many different variables (time, weather, day of week, size of rewards, gender, age, region, income and so much more), in real time every day, and being able to influence those outcomes with a tiny tweak of a reward offer, was enormously fulfilling for me.

Soon enough, all this early momentum and energy spawned some fascinating questions about our future. If Carrot was so effective (and efficient) at influencing the physical health of Canadians, why stop there? Could we also make a difference in areas like mental health? Should our mission be broadened to other forms of wellness, like financial literacy, environmental awareness, civic engagement and active transportation? The answers were obvious to all my passionate and proud colleagues, who wasted no time connecting with policy-makers and promoters in all those areas, and before we knew it, the menu of topics on our beautiful app was exploding. Our founding friends at the Public Health Agency of Canada were proudly supporting the spreading of our platform wings, and our users across the country apparently loved the expanding variety of content on their favourite app. The possibilities suddenly were limitless.

When one of the country's largest insurance companies approached us about using Carrot to support healthier lifestyles among their customers, we realized that many more collaboration opportunities existed for us beyond our original government partners. Public wellness isn't only important to policy-makers in government—it can be a huge differentiator for a great many private sector companies who want (or even need) all of us to live healthier and longer, to be smarter with our money, to be better-educated energy consumers and so on. As long as we stayed vigilant about protecting the authenticity of our content and the purity of our relationship with our users, we could easily accelerate our success and our influence on the lives of Canadians by allowing private sector money to boost the work that our public sector clients had been steering so successfully through Carrot.

This new direction was a little less familiar and comfortable for some of our core government partners at first, but it wasn't long before we started testing programs with corporate clients—and there was no stopping us after that. It made so much sense to be harnessing the appetite and funding of the private sector to accelerate the positive impact we were having on so many lives.

Our secret sauce for being able to grow so quickly and in so many directions was, of course, our magical team of real people. I often refer to them as "real" because the one thing that bonded us all so perfectly and made us so completely different from any other grouping of co-workers was how genuinely everyone embraced the dream. I had never before seen a company where not a single contributor treated their job as just a job; every "Carroter," as we proudly called ourselves, came to work every day for Carrot. The rest—all the stuff that conventional companies work so hard to support, like employee satisfaction, motivation, inspiration, collaboration and avoidance of politics—all that happened automatically in our gorgeous shop. Everyone was so absorbed by our collective North Star that there were absolutely no agendas, no politics, no grumpy non-contributors, no wasted energy of any kind. We were all building, all the time. And the fun factor was also like nothing I had ever experienced—every single day, we laughed and loved and we infected everyone around us with our crazy Carrot energy. Our government clients couldn't wait to get invited to Toronto for meetings with us, and our parties, planned or unplanned, always felt like family fiestas.

We started working out of one of those typical shared-office places, which are ideal for solo professionals, entrepreneurs or tiny start-ups. First we rented a little room, then a second and a third and a fourth. In less than a year we had grown to more than a dozen happy, noisy dreamers, and it was obvious that we needed (and could afford) our own space, with fewer walls and much more of that Carroter culture. A self-anointed committee of my young colleagues quickly found our new home, we signed the lease, and we got all excited about the big move—except for one funny twist: there was a one-month gap between the expiry of our original office lease and the start of the new one. We couldn't stretch either one of them to close that gap, so we suddenly needed to find a temporary place for our loud, busy gang to hang out for that month! There were plenty of hosts and companies that wanted our money and our unique energy, but none felt like the right fit, so my colleagues came up with their own solution that, frankly, was the ultimate match to the founder's quirkiness: they proposed that we spend the month working out of my home, partly to save money and partly to give us all a belated opportunity to experience that legendary thrill of a company that began in the founder's garage. I couldn't believe it! Joe couldn't believe it, when I finally summoned the courage to ask for his permission. And my colleagues, the very architects of the idea, couldn't believe it when Joe and I agreed to it.

And so our house started filling up with laptops, phone chargers, flip charts, noise, laughter and an incredible amount of new energy. Some days, when the external tech development consultants would also show up for meetings, there would be as many as twenty people scattered all over the house. Every chair, every sofa, every corner of the garden was being used for something. One day I found three people in our bedroom, sitting on the edge of our bed, participating in a conference call with clients. Another time I found a pair on another conference call inside our walk-in closet, one of the few spaces in our open-concept home that had a door. There was also the food—the piles and piles of food that kept arriving every single day. We spent most of the rent money we had saved that month on catered meals and massages for the "homeless" troops, creating truly unprecedented mountains of garbage around our home, which eventually even attracted rats to our garbage shed! It was a very special time for all of us (and for those hungry rats, I'm sure) and it added even more of that special family flavour and fuel into our dreamy venture.

And then came the most important and most essential growth moment of all: launching the app into our giant home province of Ontario. Without Ontario, which would give us both credibility and critical scale, the business would have struggled to survive in the long term. But from the very start we knew that our own province would represent a bigger challenge for us. Even though it was so much easier for us to walk up the road and meet with the appropriate officials, our conversations with them stretched a lot longer than with others. I knew the health minister personally, and we had all sorts of fans in the premier's office as well, but none of that helped to accelerate a decision.

Complicating things further was the evidence of our success in the other provinces. It was easy for us to project how many Ontarian hearts would be stolen by our beautiful app, but that huge number of hearts translated to a huge number of dollars that would be needed to fund all those daily rewards.

After many months of explorations, anxiety, anticipation and plenty of scares, I got a call one day from the health minister confirming that he had found a modest amount of funding to support a launch. I was surprised by how small the amount was and I spoke to him candidly about how this money would only last for a few months. I asked him if he thought we should wait a little bit longer to allow him to find more funding. I also made it clear that if we launched and then the funding ran out and we were all forced to abruptly stop offering wellness rewards to hundreds of thousands of Ontarians, this could become a serious public relations problem for his government and an existential crisis for my young business. He said he understood all that but suggested we get started right away and figure out the rest later. His comments made me feel reasonably confident that things would ultimately work out and he would find ways to continue funding us once the program became successful. So, we made the decision to launch.

The app proved just as popular in Ontario as it had elsewhere—which, of course, meant that the absolute number of users in our home province exploded much faster than anywhere else. When we were planning a media event near the provincial legislature to announce the arrival of Carrot, we (naively, perhaps) offered a small number of points to our early Ontario users as an enticement to come out to the event and create a small, cheering crowd for us. We assumed that perhaps a couple of hundred Torontonians would take time in the middle of a busy work day to show up just to earn those few points, but when we saw over two and a half thousand advance registrations, we realized we were facing a real crowd management issue and even considered notifying the police. We scrambled to find a much larger space, and ended up with something that looked much more like a large and loud political rally than a media announcement.

Hundreds of thousands of Ontarians had jumped on our Carrot app right away and were happily collecting points every day as they learned to live healthier lives. But from the start, we could see that we were quickly headed towards the moment when the health minister's original budget would run out. The approaching cliff presented us with a stark choice: once we had exhausted that tiny budget from the government, should we start paying for all the daily rewards ourselves, or just shut down the whole program in Ontario?

Both options were terrifying. If we had to foot the bill for the billions of rewards points that were being devoured by our fellow citizens, we would drive our dreamy little business right into bankruptcy. If, on the other hand, we chose the "safe" route and shut down the program in Ontario while we waited for new funding, we would do irreparable damage to our relationship with the hundreds of thousands of passionate people who had become used to our daily nudges.

We knew the only realistic scenario was to quickly find a way to extend our original deal with the minister. We worked hard to infuse some sense of urgency into his massive and slow-moving bureaucracy, but nothing seemed to work. We tried every kind of approach and every angle, meeting dozens of times with his officials, speaking directly and bluntly with him, even escalating our concerns all the way to his boss, the premier. The responses from every corner were remarkably (and frustratingly) similar: "we're looking into it," "we're working on it" or "please tell us more and send us more evidence."

The closer we got to that cliff, the tougher it became for my colleagues to muzzle me and control my public musings about the inaction and foot-dragging among our government clients. It all seemed so unfair, so unnecessarily slow and so short-sighted to me, and I felt like grabbing a megaphone and screaming about it from the rooftops. Couldn't they see how they were about to wreck a unique, world-leading program that was clearly having a positive effect on hundreds of thousands of lives? Didn't they care that our young and proud social venture would go up in smoke because of their indecisiveness? The closer we got to that cliff, the more unfiltered I became and the more work it took for my colleagues to smooth my sharp edges.

Then we woke up one summer morning and found we had gone over the cliff. The Ontario government money had run out. Nobody was there any more to pick up the tab for those couple of points that half a million of our fellow citizens would earn that day just for walking a few extra steps. That was the day we became the corporate equivalent of the frog that slowly boiled itself to death.

We didn't shut down the program, because we thought it made more sense to continue to keep our passionate users fully engaged for another day while we fought for funding. We chose not to destroy all that value for the sake of a few extra thousand dollars' worth of reward points. And we thought and did the same thing the next day—just a few more thousands of dollars' worth of patience. And the same the day after that. We kept going and trying and slowly boiling, day after day, week after week, month after month. For eight long months after that miserable "cliff day," right until the moment the government lost the election and it became certain that our bills would never get paid, we kept hoping for funding while gradually sinking ourselves into an unimaginable financial abyss. By the end of that long slow boil, our tiny social venture had outspent its very own gigantic government many times over.

All through that long, ugly slide we faced an even bigger challenge: we couldn't attract any investment into Carrot.

With such a huge unknown hanging over us, investors wouldn't touch us until they understood exactly what would happen to our growing Ontario liability. Hopeful statements didn't count; the only thing that would matter in the end was certainty (good or bad) about those invoices that we kept sending to the Ministry of Health. There was no other way for an investor to figure out what Carrot was worth and why they should put money into it. So we kept going through that long, ugly, eight-month slide with little money in the bank and even less investment hope on the horizon.

If we hadn't been blessed with the world's most patient suppliers, who kept letting us stretch the money we owed them for all those points that Ontarians were devouring through the program every day, we wouldn't have lasted long at all. The biggest star among those patient suppliers was, once again, Matthew Seagrim—the same genius in charge of the very popular Scene program, who had believed in us and stood by us right from the start.

Writing off our unpaid Ontario bills once the government fell was obviously very painful—but at least we finally had some certainty. We were quickly able to start looking for investors to help us start growing again. The conversations were not easy, considering the financial ugliness and the dashed hopes of the previous months. We needed to move fast. We tried to do this by limiting ourselves to potential investors who already knew us, but in fact the opposite happened—by letting ourselves get backed into a corner, with no alternatives or leverage, weeks turned into many months, deals proved incredibly elusive, handshakes and promises became impossible to translate into contracts, and friendships began to melt.

I became unrecognizable. Never before in my career had I dealt with so much intensity and such deep stress over such a long period of time. For the first time in my life I stopped sleeping well. It became impossible to smooth my autistic edges and filter my communication, particularly with those whose style or values didn't match mine. I was having such a tough time reconciling the behaviour of those who only knew how to optimize money with everything that was going on in my heart, my soul and my unique social venture. We were so used to building dreams and wanted to continue changing lives; they only cared about financial returns. Carrot had been created as the perfect marriage of those two worlds, a social venture that would make more and more money as it effected more and more lives. But with our post-Ontario debts piled up high, venture capitalists were in no mood to talk about anything other than safe returns, at the cost of absolutely everything else.

Those many months of needing to talk from just one side of our mouths, focusing only on money and never on impact, were so ugly and dark for me. I felt I had no choice, but for the sake of keeping our dream alive, I somehow kept muddling through it inauthentically. It was a period of unprecedented disillusionment.

The way my Carrot team gelled together through that incredibly stressful period was reminiscent of how my Green Rewards colleagues had stuck it out with me through that scary summer a decade earlier, when the floor had collapsed beneath us on the cancelled BMO acquisition deal. Instead of panicking, checking out or blaming, they solved, built and celebrated all our good fortune. Every time I stood in front of them and gave them the latest update on our slow boil, all I could see was the passion and the pride in their faces—and I constantly felt overwhelmed by gratitude for having all those special believers and dream builders with me.

While our Ontario funding gap was growing and our investors' angst was consuming us, what grew even faster was the prominence of our story. We had gone from being a project and a company that needed explaining to a brand that everyone recognized. In our early days, when the person next to me on a plane asked me what I did, I would need to start my response by describing our platform as an idea or a shy experiment. Ontario changed all that for us because most of our country's national media are centred in Toronto, and once the journalists knew and loved Carrot, everyone did. The new version of the plane seatmate exchange was now much shorter. I would simply say, "I run Carrot," and their eyes would instantly light up. For so many, it was suddenly a big deal to be chatting with the founder of one of the most popular apps in the country. One of the hidden benefits of having an autistic mind is that you thrive on simple, binary situations and conversations, and being able to answer that question in three words, instead of having to describe something functionally, made me a much more comfortable seatmate. Not to mention my hubby's endless pride, of course, which always served as my most effective rocket booster. He would watch those fun reactions to my three-word answer at cocktail parties and his face would beam. That shy little idea that had begun somewhere in our home—deep inside my belly, as I always said—had become a prominent, real, national brand. The more he smiled proudly, the farther I felt I could fly.

Speaking of flying, the next natural frontier for our proud project was to start inspiriting other countries and their governments with the idea. Not surprisingly, London was calling first. In fact the U.K. had never really stopped calling, ever since the humble days of our trying to deflect and nurture the Carrot concept elsewhere while steering clear of all the legal restrictions after my Air Miles divorce. One of my original co-founders lived in Britain and never stopped trying to plot our path to launch in that country. Once our Canadian success story exploded and our public impact became so clearly visible, the path to replicating Carrot in that country became much clearer and the pace accelerated dramatically.

The ultimate architect of our UK launch was a man named Michael Ekpe, who reminded me of Rodney—same style, wisdom, passion and exceptional ability to navigate complex and inertia-filled government corridors. Michael was in charge of technology for Public Health England and he managed to raise the profile of Carrot in record time, all the way to the British Prime Minister's Office, where he eventually got the highest official blessing for this bold move. Almost unbelievably, the way he shared the happy decision with me was practically identical to the way Rodney had communicated our Canadian government's approval three years earlier: he tried calling but couldn't get hold of me because it was still the middle of the night in California, where I had been at a conference, eight time zones away from London. He then resorted to sending me a text message, beginning with that now familiar line, "I really wanted to share the happy news live, by phone," which I saw just as I was packing my bags to fly home. And as if that wasn't enough of a coincidence, this all happened on the fortieth birthday of my Carrot board chair, significant investor and very close friend Irfhan Rawji, who was also at that conference with me.

Sometimes I close my eyes and try to rewind this movie. After I sold my last business, and especially after Joe and I got sick and became known as "survivors," I had really thought I was done. Coasting through life, sharing my story, holding the hands of younger entrepreneurs, donating my time to build a happier world—that, I thought, was the extent of my ambitions. But, as it turned out, the happiest and greatest twist of my life was yet to come—and I was so ready to embrace it and let it transform me. In the span of three fast, packed years, Carrot has completely redefined not only my life and legacy but also my ambitions, my future energy and my self-perception. I no longer see myself as an accidental one-time entrepreneur—the one that overcame the odds stacked against him, the strange autistic guy who somehow managed to sneak through only once to build something. That was so three years ago. The new interpretation of me, by me and by those close to me, involves much more boldness and pride and much more conviction that there's no better jet fuel than the things that make us different. The first three incredible years of Carrot redefined me and reshaped the story in this book.

AGE

WHEN I WAS A TODDLER I would start crying as soon as I heard the spoon hit the bottom of my dinner bowl, because that would be the first sign that the joy of that great meal wouldn't last forever.

When I grew a little older, I noticed that I preferred westbound flights, because when you chase the sun across time zones, time practically stands still and days seem to last forever, while on eastbound flights the clock moves twice as fast. I never liked it when an entire day would essentially vanish off the calendar because I was flying east, but I cherished those never-ending days of flying from Athens to London to Toronto to Winnipeg and then taking a bus to Brandon. Twenty-four hours later, it would still be the same happy day.

Time has always been my most anxiously guarded asset. My neuro-atypical and numerically charged mind has never stopped feasting on the value, the beauty and the scarcity of it. I've never been able to live without a watch, and I've never been able to tolerate all those age-neutralizing clichés: "You're only as old as you feel," "Age is just a number" and so on. I know, I feel, I understand and I appreciate age in ways others find bizarre, fascinating, tiring and (most often) annoying.

I created the first edition of this little memoir around the numerical midpoint of my adult life. Even though the number wasn't ever particularly pretty or meaningful to me, I had always considered the age of fifty a significant milestone. There's all the great stuff about being at the peak of life, about the magnificent combination of energy and perspective and about the blend of endless opportunities and freedom. But, mathematically speaking, it was also going to be the first time that the big spoon would start hitting the bottom of the precious bowl. Life would begin to feel more like an eastbound flight, and my calculator brain would start to obsess over the realization that there is less runway ahead of me than behind me.

My age-defying and radically nonconformist mother dropped dead without warning at sixty. I was devastated not only by the enormous shock of losing her but also by the illogical and uncontrollable realization that my own reverse clock had just been started. I could easily calculate the number of days left until I would reach that same age, and I almost started assuming that my natural expiration date might be the same as hers. But the abrupt introduction of a subconscious deadline also imbued life and time with a new preciousness. Suddenly, each day had to matter; it wasn't good enough anymore to just wake up and live an ordinary day. Instead, the fast-ticking clock made it essential to maximize the fun, the human connections, the love and, above all, the impact.

Impact. The notion of it went from somewhere deep in my subconscious to the very top of my mind and parked itself there permanently. It became synonymous with wealth: if I have the ability and power to touch, influence and change something that matters in the world around me, then I feel rich. It may have been easier in my younger years to merely exist, enjoy, observe and learn, but it feels as if life became meaningful only when I grew up enough to be capable of influencing others. From being able to hold the hands of those I teach and mentor to having the power to create businesses that defy paradigms and bring real change to our society, my grown-up definition of wealth is remarkably different from anything I used to imagine before. Now, that reverse clock isn't quite as intimidating, and the daily search for meaning isn't nearly as anxious. Time and its ugly modern-era sister, money, no longer dominate me the way they once did. I am no longer expected to "arrive"; the fulfillment is in what happens along the way. And life is so much more beautiful this way.

One of the greatest side effects of this healthy shift of attention from the destination to the journey was the arrival of a very sweet new friend: nostalgia. Autistic, escapist, immigrant-by-choice, misfit boy didn't have any time or need for her before. Sure, she would tease me once in a while—the occasional smell of a fig may have reminded me of Monemvasia; I may have caught a glimpse of a country road that brought a flashback to those crazy student road trips in Manitoba; and the sound of my dad's voice on some old recording may have triggered a brief burst of emotion. But those were fleeting little moments and memories, and I didn't really know what I was supposed to do with them.

They were simply there, and they were already mine anyway, so I just kept leaving them on the shelf. And then, when life started to change from a race to a project, all those memories became amazing assets, and deep, genuine nostalgia suddenly became a powerful force and a real enabler for me to inspire and change others.

I've been blessed with an enormous bank account of diverse experiences and assets to draw from: life on two continents; nearly a dozen bizarre micro-careers; exposure to some of the leading minds of our world; a twisted, neuro-atypical, uncomfortable and restless mind; a gifted brother with even more of what I have. The rich cocktail of my life has real value because so many parts of it can be dredged up to enrich conversations, guide ideas, inspire new forms of trust or simply add a lot more flavour and depth to life. I found myself reconnecting more meaningfully with my people back in Greece; helping my incredible little brother figure out why and how he's so different; building a deep bond with our only surviving parent, my beautiful mother-in-law; going on dinner dates with my wise old high school teacher; and writing this book. It has all made me feel richer, definitely more useful for this world and immeasurably happier.

More than anything, I miss those who shaped me. My creative, perceptive, disruptive, irreverent, scared, addicted, frustrated and often lonely mom still lives in me, in so many ways—I miss her unconditional pride in me, no matter how awkwardly and infrequently she expressed it. My imposing, frightening, frustrating, unbending, isolating dad—I miss him stretching me in so many ways; I miss our debates and the continuous drip of wisdom; I miss his unspoken appreciation of the other; and, perversely, I really miss that perpetual and aggravating effort to simply impress him.

The peak of life is an extraordinary place. I don't feel tired, even though I've covered much more distance than I would have expected. I don't feel old, even though I'm always surrounded by much younger friends and fellow dreamers. I don't feel bored or anxious, even on days or weeks when I may seem to be doing or changing little. I don't feel scared or isolated, even though the only way I know how to create change is head-on. And I don't feel egotistical, even though I've been using my story—this story—to lead and influence in very personal ways.

My biggest asset now is my age, because of everything that comes with it. I truly have no idea what the rest of the accelerating eastbound journey will look like, but I feel a thousand times stronger, wiser, more self-aware, more needed and perhaps even more curious and adventurous than I did all those years ago on that first one-way westbound flight to Canada.

CHANGE

I WROTE THIS BOOK to help inspire more change for our world. I was raised believing that I needed to change in order to fit into the world, but I didn't really grow up until I realized that the opposite was true: the world needed me to help change it a little bit.

Everyone is a misfit in some way—I just happened to be born bolder, louder, quirkier and with more jagged edges than most. Fitting into an organized human society, respecting others' boundaries, learning how to be understood and how to grow along with your tribe—those are all essential elements of survival.

But the balancing act is much tougher for those of us with the more extraordinary gaps and skills, because it's so easy for us to go overboard and get ourselves squished into crippling conformism, shyness and self-doubt.

I could have ended up living in a suburb of Athens as a completely repressed autistic and homosexual man, married to a woman and raising beautiful children. I could have had a simple and easy career as a math or piano teacher or as a computer analyst. And I could have still been enjoying a predictable paycheque by keeping my head low inside the multi-billion-dollar firm that bought my first social venture.

Any of those scenarios would have been "normal" and "good," according to some, and perhaps even easy, but would have wasted a huge slice of my genes and capabilities.

My raw story in this book is intended to inspire others, particularly those who feel they were born a little more different, to test their boundaries and figure out a more daring and creative balance between belonging to society and reshaping their world—*our* world.

I haven't created all that much change in our world yet, but at least I have established a trajectory, and that gives me confidence about what's still to come.

It took me a long time to grow up and understand what I could do differently and how I could draw others in. I may have looked like a disruptor when I got caught swimming on that school trip or when I was inventing my first job, but deep inside I was always really shy and scared.

For far too long I felt too different, too hampered by my inability to fit in properly and too lucky to be sitting at that executive boardroom table or to be loved by the world's most genuine spouse.

I now feel proud and hungry. Proud to be infecting countless young people with stories about the thrill of change, the importance of harnessing unique genes and skills, the joy of being driven by uncompromising conviction, and the real wealth of passionate leadership. And hungry, deeply hungry, for the snowball effect ahead.

Now that I know who I am and how I can find my own unconventional route to the next peak, now that I've figured out what to do with the kind of world I see through my unique lens, now that I'm no longer afraid of labels and unreasonable rules, I can shape bigger dreams, rally bigger thinkers, create bigger disruption and create a lot more meaningful change around me.

EXTRAS

GOOSEBUMPS

BECAUSE OF THE WAY my numerically obsessed mind works, I organize memories and emotions according to timelines. Everything is slotted into a very long line of dates, and this makes it easier for me to be able to recall, organize and summarize the most significant points in my life.

Here is a sampler of those highlights—a not so random chronology of goosebumps-inducing moments from the past four decades:

#1—October 1978:
Seeing the distant, endless line of coastal lights of the city of Istanbul as we were approaching on a ship. It was to be my first of many visits to a metropolis that had acquired truly mythical status in my young mind. I had read and heard so much about its past global glory, as the capital city of the Byzantine (Greek) Empire for well over a thousand years and as the most significant part of my genetic and cultural roots. It seemed so massive from a distance, so significant,

so foreign and so intimidating. "The City," as Greeks still referred to it. The centre of the world for so many, for so long.

#2—*July 19, 1981:*

Seeing my dead grandfather, the much gentler, sweeter father figure in my young life, as they opened his casket one last time before lowering it into the grave. My first experience with permanent loss. My first heartbreak.

#3—*February 1982:*

Dialing into a gay hotline that was discreetly advertised in the student paper at Brandon University. Heart pounding. Timidly and carefully responding to questions. Relief, anxiety and disappointment that I wouldn't be meeting anyone right away—all I got was an invite to a small social gathering at someone's home several weeks later.

#4—*October 7, 1985:*

The phone call, at work, from my dad, who had just borrowed and opened my blue suitcase, found that letter and finally learned who I was. The most instantaneous, uncontrollable, frightening, maturing and useful right-hand turn of my entire life.

#5—*March 1989:*

Witnessing a beheading in Saudi Arabia. Along with a dozen other fellow Canadian exporters, I was warned by our ambassador at a reception at his residence in Riyadh not to go near the central square the next day, Friday, because that's when and where they publicly executed convicted criminals. Three of us succumbed to curiosity. We were pushed to the front of the line, for better viewing, because we were so obviously foreigners and we had to experience this close up. It was horrific, and unforgettable.

#6—February 27, 1993:
Surprising my mom on her fifty-fourth birthday by revealing her brand-new apartment, which had been secretly furnished by my closest friends. From kitchen utensils to linens, furniture and even an easel for painting, they all provided whatever spares they could find so my frightened and troubled mother could walk into a perfectly set-up home. One of the most precious videos we happen to possess.

#7—March 1997:
Walking over to a business centre in a giant exhibition hall in Hanover, Germany, to pick up a fax that contained what felt like a giant job offer. It was for my first-ever senior executive gig (at Maritz) and it couldn't wait until I was back in Canada. Neither could I! It marked the beginning of one of my most significant growth spurts.

#8—April 2001:
Phoning my recently disabled friend Derek and his incredible wife, Louise, in South Africa to say that I had booked my ticket to visit and meet their newborn twin daughters,

and hearing them both break down as they started to tell me that, just moments earlier, they had decided to ask me to be the girls' godfather.

#9—*May 2001:*
Staring at that gorgeous moon in the middle of the night over Africa and suddenly realizing that I'm already spending the rest of my life with the love of my life.

#10—*August 9, 2003:*
Going on an unexpected lunch "date" with my dad, who was visiting for my fortieth, and hearing him tell me, seriously and very nervously, that I am so fortunate to have someone in my life who loves me so much. He had spent the previous two hours patiently watching Joe prepare all sorts of banners and decorations for my birthday party that evening. He made as little eye contact as possible through that unbelievable conversation. And he was gone from this world not long after that.

#11—*July 20, 2005:*
Watching the massive media coverage of the legalization of same-sex marriage in our country. Now this really was my country.

#12—*September 2, 2008:*
Signing my name more times than I had ever imagined, as we worked through the longest, neatest arrangement of colour-ordered legal binders in a giant boardroom of a giant

corporate law firm for the sale of my Green Rewards business to Air Miles. It felt like a movie set.

#13—*November 4, 2008:*
Listening to the response of the giant, gentle, older black doorman at my hotel in Chicago when I returned from Barack Obama's victory speech at Millennium Park, shook his hand and told him how happy I was for him and for the world. He looked at me with teary eyes and said: "Sir, do you know how long I've waited for this?"

#14—*March 31, 2012:*
Dancing with my friend Justin Trudeau in a loud bar in Ottawa's ByWard Market right after his spectacular win at a charity boxing match against a beefy Canadian senator. The room was overflowing with optimism. And then Justin jumped up on stage, grabbed the mic and started to sing that crazy '90s hit: "I get knocked down, but I get up again . . ."

#15—*February 2014:*
Opening a personal letter from the president of the University of Calgary, letting me know that *Misfit* in its original version had been selected as the recommended reading for all their new students the following year, as a way of encouraging diversity of thought and mutual acceptance.

#16—*March 2014:*
Looking down at Greek parliamentarians and city mayors as I spoke about inclusiveness and brain drains, at their

country's first-ever conference on diversity. Most appropriately, the Government of Canada was the main sponsor of the event, and I was their chosen speaker. Life's full circles . . .

#17—*March 31, 2014:*

Coming back from Athens to find Joe in the middle of a heart attack. The most extreme feeling of helplessness and the closest I've ever come to praying.

#18—*January 26, 2015:*

Reading Rodney's email message, as Joe and I were boarding our flight back from Costa Rica, about Canada's health minister having just approved the launch of Carrot.

#19—*March 3, 2016:*

Sitting next to Sarah in the basement cafeteria of the British Columbia Parliament Buildings moments after our app was turned on and just as she began to receive activity reports about the thousands who were instantly downloading it.

#20—*All the time:*

Listening to our Canadian national anthem. Uncontrollable goosebumps.

STATEMENTS

A SAMPLER OF THE THINGS I've said publicly, passionately and sometimes shamelessly.

An Open Letter to the Prime Minister of Greece

Published in the *Huffington Post*, August 28, 2014.

> The Hon. Antonis Samaras,
> Prime Minister of the Hellenic Republic
>
> Honourable Prime Minister:
>
> As you may be aware, earlier today a member of your national parliament and recent founder of the Greek Christian-Democratic Party used an extremely derogatory term (the Greek equivalent of the word "faggot") in a Twitter reference to the Prime Minister of Luxembourg. Apparently your fellow parliamentarian's

tweet was nothing more than an expression of his profound disapproval of the Luxemburgian Prime Minister's engagement to his same-sex partner.

As a proud expatriate Greek, living in a society where bigotry is broadly condemned, I was disappointed but perhaps not entirely shocked by your colleague's remark. Having escaped the pervasive and often overt homophobia of Greece in search of a fairer society where I could also have the right to do what your Luxemburgian counterpart did, I am not surprised by such offensive expressions. I did, however, see this particular outburst as a unique opportunity for an enlightened leader to trigger a process of positive reflection and genuine dialogue among the citizens of my beautiful birth country.

You see, Prime Minister, while a vocal minority of modern-day Greeks may be already expressing their disdain and embarrassment over your colleague's offensive remark, a very large silent majority of your fellow citizens will go to bed tonight entirely unconcerned and unaffected by today's incident. Their reaction, if they even heard or read about your colleague's public slur, would range from complete apathy, because apparently the country has more serious issues to grapple with, to thinly disguised support for that bigoted MP's views. And that is precisely where a terrific leadership opportunity lies for you: If you were to express your disappointment and communicate your genuine remorse to your Luxemburgian counterpart on behalf of an entire nation, you would automatically trigger that important adult conversation among your citizens. You would help expose and challenge some of their thinly disguised prejudices; you would start a more intelligent dialogue about some of the less obvious causes of Greece's brain-drain and brand-drain; and you would be using a small dose of national shame to begin a snowball of a debate on what it means to be a truly democratic nation, based on the ancient Greek definition of freedom.

Bigotry is not easy to erase and it will certainly take a while to enrich an entire nation with the same fundamental values of equality and unconditional mutual respect which define and guide some of the more advanced Western democracies like the one I chose to make my home. But today's incident was a perfect example of an opportunity to at least start that process. The power of your elected office, combined with a strong dose of moral courage on your part, can be harnessed to trigger a national dialogue. And once people start talking and reflecting, the layers of bigotry will gradually fall away.

Good luck, Prime Minister. This could well be one of the simplest and most rewarding leadership opportunities of your tenure. By shaming, exposing and ultimately reducing intolerance in modern Greek society, you would be honouring our proud ancient democratic heritage while also creating a unique legacy for yourself.

Respectfully,
Andreas Souvaliotis
Toronto, Canada

Why I Left Greece

Published in the *Huffington Post*, May 13, 2013.

On an early morning bike ride this week I saw a grumpy-looking older man walk out of his house, reach into his pocket, pull out an empty pack of cigarettes and toss it out onto the street.

The extra endorphins that were flowing through my body at that moment helped quickly replace my initial anger with a whole bunch of reflection. That grumpy-looking man's act felt so uncomfortably familiar. It reminded me of all the disillusionment I used to feel as a dreamy teenager growing up in a very selfish, immature, unbalanced and fundamentally undemocratic society. It reminded me of why I chose to leave Greece and move to Canada thirty years ago.

Back when I was a kid my birth country wasn't the land of debt defaults and massive layoffs, but it was already a very strange and extremely individualistic society. Modern Greeks have a unique reputation for their passion, pride, resourcefulness and entrepreneurialism; but they've also been notorious for their intense self-righteousness and their perpetual inability to hold themselves accountable. In the country I grew up in, you were often laughed at if you were courteous to others, if you obeyed all the traffic rules or if you paid your taxes. You had no chance of success if you didn't know how to cheat and how to look after yourself first. There was no sense of common good—in fact, the "what if everyone else did this" line hardly made any sense to most of my compatriots.

Fast-forward three decades and now that society is in a full-blown crisis—affecting not just them but, in many indirect ways, the rest of us as well. Their "us first" mentality; their superficial and twisted interpretation of democracy; their Teflon pride and intense desire to blame anyone but themselves—it's all caught up to them and they're having an impossibly difficult time under-standing why and how it all happened. A majority of Greeks are still asking their government to back away from the painful austerity measures, despite knowing that it would put their nation on an express route to a disorderly bankruptcy. The pain and humiliation of the past few years don't seem to have had an effect on their national mentality yet—they still think and behave as if they deserve more, as if their well-being does not depend on anyone or anything else around them . . .

Even in their happier days, when everything seemed to be going their way and they had become a nation of experts at living beyond their means, the citizens of Greece weren't necessarily any happier than the rest of us. Finding a way to toss your pack of cigarettes onto the street, where the rest of us will have to pick it up, doesn't necessarily make life any easier for you—because in that kind of world you're probably also having to worry about your neighbors dumping their garbage on your lawn. Having to stay one step ahead of the system and one trick ahead of the next guy might be stimulating but it doesn't make life any more rewarding. That grumpy-looking man this week didn't appear to be all that happy, even though he was beating the system.

And, most ironically or perhaps appropriately, that grumpy-looking man came out of a house in Toronto's Greektown.

Au revoir, Pierre

Written in September 2000 on hearing the news of the death of Pierre Trudeau, my original source of Canadian patriotic inspiration and one of my earliest leadership idols. This is the "letter" that, years later, triggered my friendship with his son Justin.

Pierre Elliott Trudeau, the only man I never met
who had such an incredible impact on me, is gone.

Pierre was a Canadian, like I am now. His definition of our values, as a nation, made me want to be a
Canadian—and eventually made be proud to be one.
Of my nearly twenty years here, he only really ran the
country for less than three; yet those three were more
than sufficient to instill and cultivate the most genuine
sense of national pride in me.

Without trying all that hard, he taught me all about
the real beauty of a "just society." He showed me how
to challenge anything, if the goal and the logic was
there to support me. He proved to me that leaders
can really make an incredible difference—as long as
they have passion and conviction. He gave me some
of the most essential ingredients for the rest of my life
in Canada, just by defining the beauty of this country
for me. He truly helped make Canada the most just,
balanced, liberal, progressive and, more than anything,
genuine society on the planet.

All that, and yet he also taught me how not to get

too serious about anything in life. He was a model
of humour and necessary sarcasm; he was beautifully
dismissive of fools or small-minded adversaries; he
always swam upstream; and he always found spicy and
entertaining ways of challenging unreasonable tradition
or authority. A tiny little bit of eccentricity was the final
key ingredient.

If I now feared that nobody else could ever lead and
inspire the way he did, then I think his work on me
wouldn't be complete; the truth is that Pierre showed
me, and many others like me, how leaders lead . . . and
helped pave a path full of inspiration, passion and a little
bit of humour for future leaders in our society.

Au revoir, dear teacher and friend I never met.

What Leaders Can Learn from Margaret Thatcher

Published in the *Huffington Post*, April 9, 2013, the day after the death of the former British prime minister. This is me venting about all the confrontation-averse, ineffective leaders I had encountered in my life and career, particularly in the mainstream corporate world.

"Polarizing": that was the one word that really stood out in all the news reports and editorials about Margaret Thatcher's death. More than two decades after having been pushed out of office and so many years after fading from the spotlight, she still only had fans or foes. She was loved or hated—and there was no middle ground.

Thatcher was determined, driven, uncompromising, single-minded, outspoken, stubborn, intolerant, sharp, quick and unquestionably capable of evoking only intense emotions among her friends and enemies. And that's exactly why she was one of the greatest leaders of the past century, regardless of how much we may disagree with her decisions and her values.

In an interview about the controversial legacy of his good British friend, former Canadian prime minister Brian Mulroney suggested that if a leader left office on a wave of popularity, he or she probably didn't accomplish very much. I think Mr. Mulroney's assertion was bang-on. Great leaders are great simply because they make a real difference. They drive change. They're guided so sharply by their own vision, their passion and often their stubbornness. They may not always be right and they may even be terrible consensus-builders (Madam Thatcher proudly admitted that about herself!) but they're incredibly good at finding ways to push stuff through. What truly sets them apart is that they're never afraid to confront. Thatcher was never afraid. Jack Welch, Winston Churchill, Steve Jobs and Pierre Trudeau all shared that exact same attribute—they had absolutely no fear of confrontation. They all prodded and angered and disrupted—and that's exactly why and how they were able to create so much change in our world. That's why we think of them as great leaders, even if we don't agree with everything they did.

We don't celebrate great technocrats, great appeasers, great conformists or great people-coddlers because, when you think about it, they don't really change our world. They're absolutely essential and they're good at keeping the lights on for us. We've all worked with these nice unremarkable types and we've loved and respected them, but they never made our blood boil.

It was Thatcher and Welch and Churchill and Jobs and Trudeau who made us feel alive—because they didn't just keep the lights on for us; they actually turned them on, or off, they installed them, they changed them and they showed (or told) us how to use them properly! They made us question things, they made us proud and anxious and angry. And, whether we admit it or not, they inspired us.

Maggie Thatcher's political legacy was controversial, but her leadership was exceptional.

Ich Bin ein Istanbuler

Published in the *Huffington Post*, March 3, 2013.

I spent the past week at the world's largest-ever gathering of CEOs in Istanbul, Turkey. The conference involved more than two and a half thousand influential members of the twinned Young Presidents' and World Presidents' Organizations, exploring global issues with some of the best-known corporate and political leaders from across the world.

This year we were hosted by an incredibly ambitious, sophisticated, booming and proud city of more than 15 million people—Europe's largest urban metropolis and, in fact, the only mega-city on the old continent. Istanbul is often described as the place where East meets West both literally, as the world's only city that straddles two continents, and metaphorically, as perhaps the world's busiest intersection of cultures, religions and leadership styles. The city oozes optimism and a healthy kind of hunger for the future. Its exceptionally deep heritage is perfectly blended with the great energy of its educated, worldly and remarkably young workforce into one of the most powerful and attractive urban "brands" most of my fellow conference attendees had ever seen.

We all marveled at its relentless economic boom (it was barely touched by the global financial crisis), its spectacularly blossoming infrastructure, its gorgeous palaces and heritage buildings and the totally captivating attitude of its people. But for me this time Istanbul also triggered a much more personal feeling of belongingness and pride.

My grandmother was born and raised in Istanbul at the dawn of the 20th century. Back then the world still knew it as "Constantinople," the glorious old capital of the long-defunct Byzantine Empire. It had reigned as the largest and richest and coolest city on the planet for more than a thousand years (imagine a combo of Shanghai, New York, Paris and London—for a millennium?!) and there was still plenty of blue blood and matching attitude flowing through its veins, even though it was steadily sinking towards third-world oblivion by then. Like all good Greek Constantinopolites, Grandma could trace her ancestry to some distant little corner of an imperial palace, she could always blend a bit of aristocratic French into her everyday language, she could cook like a Parisian chef and she could dress like a royal. And, like most good Greek Constantinopolites, she ended up fleeing her city and became a poor immigrant in Greece. She never really let us feel her bitterness—but her impeccable style, her distinguished language and her stories about "The City," as most Greeks still refer to it, contained such intense nostalgia for a time that was obviously gone forever. I was raised in a country and a society that was still missing its city, still wishing it could have it all back someday . . .

So there was the grandson of the deposed city-princess, walking in her old neighbourhood, looking at her old school and her old church and feeling nothing but pride. I felt so blessed to be able to trace some of my roots to this gorgeous, happening, smiling place. I felt so touched, in a very Canadian inclusive and multicultural way, each time our beautiful Turkish hosts talked to us with such genuine passion about their city's Byzantine glory days, each time I heard them celebrate its deep multicultural heritage and link it all to its great new success today. And I felt so at home in a city that looks out to the future with so much optimism, so much energy and so much confidence.

My grandmother's city is definitely back. It may have a different name today, it may speak a little less aristo-cratic French and Greek, but it sure deserves and draws the world's attention again with its hot new brand and its great new language of success! And it feels so good to be a small part of it all . . .

When the Oil Stops Flowing

Published in the *Huffington Post*, April 20, 2013

I am a capitalist. In recent years I've been called a "green capitalist," and that's an accurate label, but I still absolutely believe that business and profits are core ingredients of our success as a nation and pillars of stability for our society.

I know how to count jobs and tax revenues, and I understand exactly how good the oil sands have been for my country—and specifically for me as a "shareholder" in Canada. This windfall helped us weather the deepest global recession in our lifetime better than any other rich nation and helped us pay down a very significant chunk of our national debt over the past fifteen years while also allowing us to reduce all sorts of taxes from coast to coast.

Canada has been riding this awesome wave for quite some time now—and we've become really good at it: we learned how to make the most of our new-found prosperity; how to spread it and share it almost evenly across the land; how to retool and adjust our entire economy around our much stronger petro-dollar; and how to move our skilled workers to where the action is in order to maximize our productivity and our profits. We showed the world that we're a nation of nimble, sharp, hungry capitalists, and we got a lot of respect (and envy) for that.

But while we're so good and efficient at squeezing

every available drop of profit out of our opportunities, we seem to have missed the most important lesson they teach in the School of Capitalism: strategic planning. We focused all our energy on feeding and protecting and milking our cow but forgot to plan for the day when her milk might run out or the day when people may not like that kind of milk anymore. When friends and neighbours asked us questions about the future, we got very defensive and told them we were confident nothing would ever change—the world will always need and like our milk.

And suddenly, after so many fat-cow years, our customers' tastes began to change—and, in record fast time, we behaved like the world's least sophisticated capitalists.

Suddenly it's panic season in Ottawa and in Edmonton: Will Obama approve the pipeline? Will it take us too long to get the stuff to the Chinese? Will the Europeans label our oil "dirty"? Will the world start taxing carbon?

Our finance ministers revised budgets. We started talking about (god forbid!) sales taxes even in our country's petro-province. And, of course, the blame game is now in full swing. If those tree-huggers weren't so emboldened and so well-financed by our nation's enemies, we would have plowed our pipelines right through the Rockies by now and we would have started feeding China's endless thirst for oil, instead of praying for a miracle on Pennsylvania Avenue.

We may have been the envy of the world, but we were actually amateurs all through the fat-cow years and now we're starting to pay for it. We ignored every hint of a warning and became really good at only believing ourselves.

When the rest of the planet was already contemplating or even calculating carbon taxes, we were still in total denial about the whole climate change thing—and not only were we wasting time by not planning for a different future, we were also wasting goodwill by not playing nice with all our wealthy partners (a.k.a., customers).

By ignoring or even derailing all the global conversations on carbon, we were humiliating their scientists, ridiculing their policies and frustrating their leaders—instead of reminding ourselves, as all good capitalists do, that the customer is always right. We convinced ourselves that we had become an "energy superpower" and that they needed us more than we needed them.

So now what? Do we still have an oil future? How do we navigate through this energy revolution that seems to be blossoming everywhere around us?

Thankfully, for our petro-dollar-addicted wallets at least, the world's thirst for oil is still immense—and it will stay that way for a while. We may not have the best or nicest oil on the planet, but we still have something the world needs, so the money will continue to flow our way for quite some time.

I am hopeful, however, that our intense national panic attack of these past few months will finally inspire us to pull our heads out of the oil sands and figure out how we will stay rich after the oil stops flowing.

Hopefully it will inspire us to invest our windfall a bit more wisely and strategically, instead of putting all our chips on that same number all the time. Maybe we will start to dream and lead the world a little more again—because we used to be so good at it—and maybe we will also go back to always being respectful and sensitive, the way we used to be known for so many generations, instead of being arrogant one day and then desperately subordinate a day later.

Our cow is still fat and her milk is still good and relatively popular, but we've had a real scare and I hope we learned plenty from it. We can still get richer from what we have, but we need to get serious about figuring out our future. And as good capitalists know so well, the best time to retool and invest is when the times are good.

Thirty-Five Years On

A note to myself from August 24, 2016, a moment of reflection and affirmation while visiting my birth country.

> I was scared. A gay, geeky, autistic kid in a macho, proud, homogeneous world. Total misfit, hopelessly scared, desperate for an escape.
>
> Thirty-five years ago today I ran away from the most beautiful country in the world. I missed it from the first hour. I still miss it every hour. I am constantly drawn back to it and nostalgia drives me to spend more and more time in it.
>
> On that scary August day in 1981 I made the decision to trade the most beautiful country in the world for the most beautiful society in the world. I launched a life journey that transformed me from frustrated, marginalized follower to inspired, unrestrained co-architect. I leapt from a society that had already defined my boundaries to one that actually needed my help to expand and redefine its own boundaries.
>
> My world has changed so much and yet, in some ways, so little in these 35 years. My Canada may be so much bigger, richer, more complex and more influential today but it's still the most beautiful "home" in the world. We're still the world beacon in inclusiveness, pluralism and our most distinct national value: unconditional mutual respect. We still have this magical ability to transform every immigrant and refugee that reaches our

shores into a nation-builder and a proud co-owner of our gorgeous country. And we're still an awesome, unparalleled world-magnet for scared, marginalized kids like I once was . . .

The country I left behind—the gorgeous place I'm visiting as I write this today—continues to struggle to define its relevance in the world. Despite its incredible beauty and its even more incredible cultural heritage, Greece in 2016 is just as plagued by existential anxieties as the society I abandoned as a teenager. It's still steeped in insecurities, inferiorities, hangovers and, above all, fear of the other. Time and distance has afforded me a very different and broader perspective on my birth nest, but my concerns for it haven't changed—it's a society that's still struggling to find its path. And it's a country that, sadly, drives away too many scared misfits.

I love and miss my birth nest and I so proudly "own" my chosen home country.

And I am so perfectly at peace with the conscious choice I made 35 years ago today.

THANKS

To my parents, for inadvertently gifting me with almost unlimited airspace.

To my little brother, for redefining brilliance and helping me grow.

To Sophie Grégoire and Justin Trudeau, for believing in the beauty of our world of misfits.

To Adrienne Clarkson and John Ralston Saul, for pulling me along so passionately.

To Kerry Harris and Danielle Crittenden-Frum, for nudging me to share this story.

And to Tim Rostron, the world's most fearless editor, for his endless faith, respect, guidance and patience.